Sarah narrowed her gaze and glanced at the tall man. How could he help her?

Sheriff Jones cleared his voice. "Here's the thing, ma'am. I got nobody who can identify you as the thief who shot Mary and stole her horse."

Sarah hiked up her chin. "That's because I didn't do it."

"Be that as it may, here's the deal. You can sit in this cell until the circuit judge from Dickinson comes around in a month or so, or. . ." The sheriff glanced at the other man, who looked at Sarah then pursed his lips and nodded.

Her heart thundered and her knees shook. No matter what the alternative was, she had to take it.

"Or you can marry up with this man and get out of jail today."

Sarah's mouth dipped down, but no words came out. Surely the sheriff couldn't be serious. Marry a stranger?

She glanced at the other man—the one who was willing to marry her. Why would he want to wed a woman he didn't know? A woman in jail, no less. He was handsome enough to marry any woman he wanted. She looked him in the eye and swallowed back her fear. He was the key to getting out of here.

VICKIE McDONOUGH believes God is the ultimate designer of romance. She is a wife of thirty-four years, mother to four sons, and a doting grandma. When not writing, she enjoys reading, watching movies, and traveling. Visit Vickie's Web site at www.vickiemcdonough.com

Books by Vickie McDonough

HEARTSONG PRESENTS
HP671—Sooner or Later
HP716—Spinning Out of Control
HP731—The Bounty Hunter and the Bride
HP747—A Wealth Beyond Riches
HP816—Wild at Heart
HP831—Outlaw Heart

Straight for the Heart

Vickie McDonough

Heartsong Presents

This book is dedicated to my long-time friend, Shirley McWilliams. Shirley was my mentor during a different time in my life and is now a great friend. She has proofed a number of my books and made some great catches with her eagle-eye. Thank you, Shirley. You've been a great blessing and encouragement to me.

A note from the Author:
I love to hear from my readers! You may correspond with me by writing:

Vickie McDonough
Author Relations
PO Box 721
Uhrichsville, OH 44683

ISBN 978-1-60260-438-4

STRAIGHT FOR THE HEART

one

Sarah Oakley glanced over her shoulder, listening for the sound of hoofbeats. How long before their uncle noticed them gone and came after them? A shudder snaked down her spine. If taking a beating would satisfy him, she could endure that for the sake of her siblings. But when he discovered what they'd done, she feared seeing them dead was the only thing that would soothe his vile temper.

Her arms ached from carrying the heavy load, a constant reminder of her foolish, impulsive decision, but it was the only way she could think to save her siblings.

They had to get away.

Far away.

"Hurry, kids. Walk faster."

"Why do you keep looking behind you, Sissy?" Beth turned and walked backward for a moment then faced forward again.

"Because she thinks Uncle Harlan will come gunning for us." Ryan pointed his index finger at Beth and pretended to shoot.

"Don't scare your sister." The girl worried far too much for a six-year-old.

Beth leaned against Sarah's leg, forcing her to slow her pace. "Sissy, I'm tired. My feet hurt."

Sarah shifted her heavy bundle to her other arm and rested a hand on her sister's head. She couldn't carry both Beth and the bag of gold coins. "It's only a mile or two farther. On that last hill we topped, I got a peek of that giant smokestack in Medora. We'll be there soon."

"But that's what you said last time."

"You're lazier than a one-legged chicken." Eight-year-old Ryan tucked his hands in his armpits and flapped his elbows up and down. *"Brock, brock!"*

Beth gasped and began to cry. "Ryan called me a chicken. Them's ugly."

Tears dripped down her sister's lightly freckled cheeks and onto her jaw. Sarah's shoulders and neck tightened. They were running for their lives, and her siblings couldn't quit bickering. She sighed and patted Beth's head. "Ryan, leave your sister alone."

Sarah glanced up at the sky, but darkening clouds blocked the sun. Lunchtime had surely passed by now, judging by the growl of her stomach. They should have left their uncle's shack first thing this morning, right after Uncle Harlan and his gang of three unkempt men rode west, but she had waited several hours, in case the men returned unexpectedly.

A cool breeze dried the sweat caused by her nervousness and the exertion of their quick-paced journey. The dusty path snaked through the thick grasslands of the Badlands. Sarah studied both sides of the trail, looking for hiding places in case she heard hoofbeats. After a moment, her gaze always settled back on the tall smokestack, which looked so out of place surrounded by nature—almost as if God knew she would need it one day.

"I can't see that big chimney." Beth wrinkled her brow and nibbled her lip.

"It's still there. You'll see it when we top the next hill."

They could easily get lost in this rugged land where few people lived. On all sides of them, rocky buttes had forced their way through the dense grass. Some buttes were round-topped and grass covered, while others were rocky and rugged. An artist's palette of color stretched out before her, but she couldn't enjoy it.

Too bad their dream of finding a home with their uncle had turned into a race to get away from him.

"Will Uncle Harlan be mad when he finds out we stole his gold?" Beth asked, glancing up at Sarah with wide blue eyes.

"He's an outlaw. He'll probably shoot us all," Ryan said. "Didn't you see the notches on his gun?"

Beth whimpered and clung to Sarah's pants, nearly pulling her uncle's big trousers off her hips. She braced the gold against her chest to free one hand and hiked up the pants she'd worn to disguise her feminine form.

Sarah glared at her brother. "You told Beth about Uncle Harlan?"

Ryan shrugged and pulled his gaze away from hers, a wry smile tilting one side of his mouth. She should have known he couldn't keep something like that a secret, especially since he'd been the one to overhear their uncle talking to his outlaw gang about the next bank they planned to rob. Sarah's stomach swirled. Her brother had thought it was a game to follow their uncle and see where he had buried his loot. Ryan didn't realize the action could have gotten him killed.

Sarah looked up at the clouds. *What's going to happen to us, Lord? Why couldn't Uncle Harlan have been as I remembered him?* She had prayed their uncle would love and protect his brother's orphaned children, but instead, they were just a nuisance to him.

She pursed her lips. Now they were running away with his bag of stolen gold.

"Since we've got so much money, I want a horse." Ryan eyed the sack in Sarah's hands.

"I'm turning the gold over to the Medora sheriff." She hoped to collect a reward that would be enough to take the three of them far away on the train so Uncle Harlan couldn't find them.

"But I found it so I should get to keep it." Ryan scowled

and tightened his hands around the canteen strap that looped over one shoulder, then his expression softened. "I could buy you a new dress."

Sarah pressed her lips together to keep from smiling. Blackmail wouldn't work on her. "The gold doesn't belong to us, you know that."

"Yeah. It's stealing if we keep it, and stealing is a sin." Beth made a face at Ryan.

He jumped in front of Sarah before she could grab him and gave Beth a shove. "Who asked you?"

Beth gasped and spun around, falling to the ground. "Ow, ow. My ankle." She grabbed her right leg and rocked back and forth.

Sarah dropped the bag of gold and the quilt she carried and knelt beside her sister, giving her brother a stern glare. What would they do if Beth was seriously injured? *Please, God. No.*

"How bad does it hurt, sweetie?"

Tears ran down Beth's face. "It hurts bad, Sissy."

Sarah closed her eyes. They'd gone too far to go back, and even if they did and reburied the gold, surely their uncle could tell it had been tampered with. They had no choice but to continue on to Medora. Sarah straightened. "Ryan, you carry the rifle and the gold."

"But that's too heavy. I can't—"

"You will." Fear that they'd be caught had already worn her nerves as thin as a paper dollar, but she had to remain strong. She reached out to Beth. "I'll carry you, and you can hold the quilt with our belongings."

In less than a half hour's time, Sarah's back and arms ached. Nearly out of breath from carrying the six-year-old, she stopped to rest as they crested the next rise. Beth was almost asleep with her head bobbing down and back up.

A jackrabbit darted across the trail and down a hill. It

dashed a few yards away then stopped beside a juniper bush. Its ears twitched. Past the rabbit, a dilapidated shack sat partially hidden in a copse of aspen and pines. If not for the rabbit, she would have walked right past the place and never seen it.

She lifted her knee and shifted Beth in her arms. She gazed toward Medora. The smokestack rose up in the distance, appearing closer than it had been earlier, but it was still a long way off. An idea formed in her mind, but just as quickly she dismissed it. Nibbling on her lip, she studied the sky. If only the clouds weren't so thick she'd be better able to determine the time of day. Maybe there was enough time—if she hurried.

No, she couldn't do it. She couldn't leave the children here and go on alone.

"Let's take a break and eat lunch in that old shack."

Beth yawned and turned her head from side to side. "Where?"

"Down there." Sarah pointed toward the structure. "We'll be out of sight should anyone ride past the trail."

They slid down the hill, sending pebbles cascading. Sarah brushed a spiderweb out of the doorway and peeked inside the shack, glad to see the layer of dirt on the floor was free of footprints. At least no people or critters had been there in a long while.

"It's dirty." Beth stared at the floor.

"And it stinks, too." Ryan wrinkled up his face.

"But it's shady and will protect us if we get rain."

Sarah set Beth down, and the girl held onto the doorframe, keeping her sore foot from touching the ground. Sarah rolled her head and shoulders, trying to work out the kinks.

Ryan plunked down the gold sack with the name of a Deadwood, South Dakota bank stamped on it. Sarah spread out the thin quilt that held their meager possessions, and her sister hopped over and plopped down. Sarah's gaze shifted back to the canvas bag and lingered a moment. Using the gold to buy the food and clothing they needed was tempting. They had done without so many basic things that others took for granted for so long now.

"No." She shook her head. Guilt would drive her crazy were she to do such a thing. The reward for returning the gold should be sufficient to give them a new start. It had to be.

"No, what?" Beth jerked her hand away from the bandana that held bread she'd been reaching for.

"Nothing, sweetie. Just talking to myself."

Ryan flopped down and tilted back the canteen. He took several long swigs.

"Go easy on the water. We don't know how long that will have to last us." Sarah untied the knot in the bandana that held their only food. She tore off chunks and gave them to her siblings. It wasn't much but would have to do until they could find something better. Too bad she didn't have time to trap and cook that rabbit.

"Is this all we get to eat?" Ryan turned up his nose at the dry bread.

"We'll get more once we get to town." If things worked out right.

Beth nibbled at her bread, her eyelids sagging. Sarah sighed and looked around. The lopsided one-room shanty was about as ramshackle as her uncle's, but it provided protection. She glanced at Beth's ankle, but the girl's shoe covered it. If she were to remove the shoe and the ankle swelled, she wouldn't be able to get it back on. Better to leave it alone.

Dare she leave her siblings here while she walked to town? They could rest, and she could hurry to Medora and turn in the gold. The three of them could hide out here until the day the train arrived. But could she leave her siblings? Even for a short time?

Ryan munched his bread and yawned. The long walk had tired him out, too. Sound asleep, Beth slumped over onto the quilt, a bit of bread still clutched in her fist. Ryan leaned back against the splintery, gray wall and closed his eyes.

Sarah gazed at her exhausted siblings and then at the crooked door. Her train of thought made her body quiver. She couldn't leave them. But she had to. There was no other choice. She could get to town and back quicker without them. The decision made, she stood.

Ryan yawned and opened his eyes. Sarah picked up the rifle and handed it to him.

"I'm going into town alone. You watch over Beth. I won't be gone too long."

"You're leaving us?" Ryan jumped up, his eyes wide.

"Beth is too tired to go on. If I go by myself, I can get to town, collect the reward, buy some food, and be back before dark."

Ryan's lower lip trembled. Sarah rested her palms on his thin shoulders. "I don't want to leave you at all, but Beth needs to sleep for a while and to rest her ankle. We can't leave her alone and there isn't enough time to wait until she wakes." Ryan needed to rest, too, but if she suggested that, he'd only balk at the idea. "You're a brave boy. I can trust you to take care of your sister."

"I'll guard her." He dropped back down and laid the rifle across his lap.

Sarah tucked her uncle's shirt into the big trousers. She patted her hair, making sure it was neatly pushed under an old felt hat. "Do I look like a man?"

Ryan shrugged and yawned. "Not to me."

Sarah untied the rope holding up her pants and redid it. "I just figured we'd be safer if folks thought I was a man with two younguns instead of a woman."

Ryan took a sip from the canteen then lay down beside Beth with his arm around the rifle. They were so young to be left alone in a strange place. Was she doing the right thing? What would Beth do when she awakened and found Sarah gone?

She couldn't waste any more time arguing with herself. "Stay hidden and do not leave here, no matter what. It'll be close to dark before I get back, and I don't want to have to go hunting for you two."

He nodded but wariness haunted his blue eyes behind his false bravado. Forcing a smile, Sarah bent and ruffled his brown hair. "Those shooting lessons I've been giving you were timely. Just be careful. Watch Beth closely, and don't fight with her."

Ryan saluted like a little soldier. Leaving them was one of the hardest things she ever had to do, but this was the best solution.

Half an hour later, Sarah stared at the gray clouds and lengthened her stride. If she didn't get to town before the storm hit she would get drenched. She shifted the gold to her other arm. *Hurry. Hurry.*

The toe of her shoe sent a rock skittering across the narrow trail. She welcomed the noise. Without the chatter of the children, the wilds of the Badlands seemed more frightening. Her gaze darted to the left and then the right. This was the first time she'd been truly alone since her parents' deaths. Only the wind and her shoes scuffling against the rocky ground made any noise. She'd kept so busy trying to keep her family together and finding food for her noisy siblings that she'd never noticed the quietness before.

On the farm there was always a dog barking, cows lowing, or chickens clucking. And there was her mother's soft humming as she worked in the kitchen. The quiet pressed in on her.

" 'Yea, though I walk through the valley of the shadow of death, I will fear no evil: for thou art with me; thy rod and thy staff they comfort me.' Walk with me, Lord. Please take these fears away."

With each step, her fear lessened. She wasn't alone. No matter what happened, God was with her.

She looked skyward again. How long since she'd left Ryan and Beth? An hour? Two?

The walk was taking far more time than she expected it would. After she turned in the robbery money, would she be able to collect a reward today? They were nearly out of food. How would they survive if they had to wait for payment of the reward?

A whinny pulled her from her thoughts. About twenty feet off the path, a horse turned to look at her. Sarah tightened her grip on the gold. She hadn't considered until now that someone else might steal it away from her. She couldn't let that happen.

"Hello? Anybody there?" The only sound was the swish of the wind in the tall grass. Sarah scanned the small valley for the horse's owner. Why would someone leave their mount untied? "Easy now, that's a good girl."

The sleek gray horse jerked its head but stood still. Its black nostrils flared and ears flicked as it watched her. The mare stuck its muzzle toward her open hand and stepped forward, and Sarah wrapped her hands around the reins. There were no human footprints in the dirt near the animal. Could the owner be injured? She climbed a large rock and cupped her hand over her eyes and searched the valley again, this time with a better view. There were no signs of another human being and no buzzards circling, indicating a person badly injured.

Maybe the horse ran off, and if that was true, she should take it back to town so that wild animals didn't harm it. With its reins dragging, the horse could easily trip or get tangled in a bush and then it would be stuck. Also, if the rider was missing, surely someone in town would recognize the mare and send a search party.

She might even get a reward for returning the pretty mare with the expensive tooled saddle. Her heart danced at the thought of what she could do with the extra money. If she rode the horse to town, she could get back to the kids even sooner.

She shoved the gold into one of the empty saddlebags, but the flap refused to close. Sarah tied it shut the best she could. The bag of coins was wedged in good and tight and wasn't going anywhere. A north wind tugged at her hat and sent gusts of cool air into the gaps on her uncle's shirt. Being so far north, even summer could be chilly at times. She tucked the shirt in, put her foot in the stirrup, and mounted the mare. "Thank you, Papa, for insisting I learn to ride astride, and thank you, Lord, for the horse."

Twenty minutes later, she passed a few shacks and then crossed the bridge over the Little Missouri River. She rode past the giant brick smokestack of an abandoned factory. The town of Medora was little more than a handful of buildings—a few brick, but most made of wood or stone—spread out in a valley sheltered by tall buttes on all sides.

Sarah rode down the wide street, looking for the sheriff's office. A man to her right shouted, and people stopped on the boardwalk. All turned to stare at her. She tugged her hat down, hoping her hair was still covered.

In the minute it took to walk the horse into town, a crowd gathered off to one side. A dozen men stood on the boardwalk outside the mercantile and barbershop. Shouts and angry voices filled the streets as the growing crowd surged toward her. Heart skittering, she glanced over her shoulder, hoping they were yelling at someone else, but nobody was on the trail behind her. She didn't understand their hostility. A thin man hurtled toward her and grabbed the reins. The mare jumped sideways and squealed at the sudden action.

"That's Mary Severson's horse." A scowling, red-faced man shook his fist at Sarah.

"*Ja*, dat vas the horse dat ran off after Mary vas shot," A tall, fair-skinned man bobbed his blond head.

Sarah's heart lurched. Had her uncle's gang robbed the Medora bank instead of the one in Wyoming like they'd planned? The shouts grew louder, and the horse pranced sideways. The crowd encircled her and closed ranks. The mare reared up, and Sarah clutched the saddle horn to keep from falling.

Big hands suddenly yanked Sarah backward off the horse. The crowd swarmed her.

A tall man grabbed the bag of gold and yanked it out of the leather saddlebags. He opened it and stared. "Look! He has the stolen gold and paper money from the bank robbery in his saddlebags."

The roar of the crowd grew louder. Sarah jerked and struggled against her captors, but she couldn't break free. They propelled her against her will toward the middle of town.

"It's not my gold. I'm returning it!" Sarah shouted, but her cries were drowned out by the crowd's frenzy.

"String 'im up!"

"Get a rope."

"Shoot him. Hanging's too good for the likes of him."

Three blasts of gunfire echoed off the surrounding hills, and the crowd instantly grew quiet. Sarah jerked toward the sound, her arms hurting where the two men on either side of her held her tight. This couldn't be happening. *Lord, help me.*

"What's going on?" A tall, middle-aged man with a thick moustache that curled on the edges stood on the elevated boardwalk holding a rifle. A badge was pinned to his vest.

"That man. He's one of the robbers who shot Mary Severson and stole her horse and robbed the bank," a deep voice behind Sarah boomed out.

"Yeah," another man called, "he was riding Mary's horse and had the gold in his saddlebags."

"That right?" The deputy scanned the crowd as they yelled their affirmation in unison. "All right then, bring him up here."

The crowd parted, and the two men holding Sarah hauled her forward.

"Let me go. I'm innocent." She fought her captors, but they were too strong. Her heart pounded and her legs trembled. Why wouldn't anybody listen to her pleas?

Surely the sheriff would be more reasonable. When he learned the truth, he would set her free. He had to let her go. She had to get back to her siblings before dark.

Please, Lord. Help me.

The men plunked her down on the boardwalk as the noise of the crowd rose again. One man shoved her toward the deputy sheriff so hard that she collided against his chest. Her hat plopped off her head, and her hair cascaded down around her face.

The crowd, a horde of smelly, bearded men, gaped in stunned silence.

❧

Quinn McFarland was so angry at his grandmother he could yank nails from a horseshoe with his bare teeth. The horse pulling the buckboard jerked its head and snorted, slowing its pace. Quinn relaxed his tight hold on the reins and clucked out the side of his mouth, urging the horse forward. He couldn't leave that poor woman alone at the depot, even if he only learned he was to marry her this morning.

But how could his grandma do such a thing without talking to him? Didn't he have any say in the matter? How does someone go about arranging a mail-order bride in the first place?

Quinn thought of how happy his twin siblings were now that they were both married. He hoped to get married one day, too, but to a woman of his own choosing, not one picked out of a catalog or a newspaper ad. And certainly not to one that his grandmother had chosen for him.

Zerelda von. . .Something, no less. He shook his head and pulled back on the reins of his temper, forcing himself to relax.

Since he moved Grandma Miles to the ranch, it seemed as if her main duty was to needle him into finding a good wife. She wanted grandchildren before she died—as if fathering a child was all he had to worry about.

"When am I supposed to find time to court a woman?" He smacked his gloved hand against his thigh. Every waking hour he'd worked hard to keep the ranch going well enough to support his family. Not that it mattered now that they'd all moved away—except Grandma.

Quinn stared at a red-tailed hawk soaring carefree in the sky. What he wouldn't give to have that bird's lack of cares. If only his mother hadn't died suddenly and he hadn't moved his grandma to the ranch, he wouldn't be in this predicament. But family cared for family. He loved his grandma but was tired of her meddling.

He steered the buggy down the hillside to Medora. The town was tucked in a cozy valley in the heart of the Badlands. Medora made a charming picture for newcomers, but life in this part of the country was tough. It took a certain kind of man— and a much stronger woman—to be able to survive the harsh winters and sometimes scorching summers, not to mention the loneliness of ranch life. Somehow he didn't think Miss Zerelda von. . .What's-her-name had it in her. She'd probably take one look at the tiny town and its lack of amenities and catch the first train back East.

Red hair, hazel eyes. That's what the letter had said. There couldn't be too many women with that coloring arriving by train in Medora. Quinn checked his pocket watch then guided the buggy toward the post office. There was time to run a few errands before he had to be at the depot to meet the afternoon train. Maybe by then he'd know if he wanted to keep the woman or send her back on the next train.

With women being few and far between out West, maybe he should accept the bird-in-the-hand. He'd make his grandma happy and get her off his back, but he'd be saddled with a woman he hadn't asked for and didn't want. Could a man come to love a mail-order bride?

Maybe she was so homely she couldn't find anyone to marry her in her hometown. Or could be she was as crotchety as a hen caught in a downpour.

He climbed out of the rig, his brain tired from arguing with himself. He hadn't done this much thinking since. . . well, he couldn't remember.

The June breeze whipped around him, hinting at cooler weather. A north wind like this could be a blessing in summer, but not so in the winter. He paused to take a swig from his canteen, but the lukewarm water did little to soothe his thirst. He returned his canteen to the wagon and entered the post office. "Afternoon, Mr. Simms. Got any mail for the Rocking M?"

"Good day to you, and yes, I believe I do." The postmaster, a thin man clad in a wrinkled white shirt and black pants, nodded his head. He turned, reached into a slot, and retrieved several letters.

Quinn took the stack and nodded his thanks. Outside on the boarded walkway, he stared at the depot. Should he keep the bride or send her back on the next train?

He watched two cowpokes chatting beside their mounts. A businessman in a suit strode down the boardwalk across the street then turned into the barber shop. Not a woman was in sight. Quinn heaved a sigh. Might as well keep the bride. It wasn't like he had many opportunities to meet women, and in two years he'd turn thirty. If he wanted to marry and start a family, the time was now. He'd just have to keep the woman. After all, it was what *she* wanted. Otherwise she wouldn't be traveling so far to marry him.

Relieved to have finally made one of the biggest decisions of his life, he thumbed through the mail. His hands stopped on one particular missive from Zerelda von Hammerstein. Ah. . .that was her name. The letter was addressed to him, so he flipped it over and opened it. He just hoped she hadn't changed her arrival date and that he hadn't wasted half a day coming to town. He shook open the single sheet of paper.

> *Dear Mr. McFarland,*
>
> *After much prayer and talking with my minister, I have come to the conclusion that to marry a stranger would be a drastic mistake for me. I hope you don't take this offensively, for it is no reflection on your character. I just can't marry a man I don't know. Please forgive me for getting your hopes up. As a result of my decision, I will not be arriving on the June 4th train. Please accept my humblest apology for any inconvenience my change of mind has caused you.*
>
> *I remain, sincerely yours,*
Zerelda Ingrid von Hammerstein

Quinn sighed. He'd been left at the altar—no, he hadn't even gotten that far. He shook his head, his self-esteem plummeting.

"I've been dumped by my own mail-order bride." A bride he hadn't wanted or even known about until his grandmother had informed him about her this morning at breakfast. And what about the funds his grandmother had mailed to the bride to pay for her trip here? The woman hadn't even been courteous enough to return the money. Quinn crumpled up the missive and tossed it at the buggy. Half a day wasted on fetching a bride who hadn't wanted him. How could her rejection sting when he'd decided to marry her just five minutes ago?

And what would he tell his grandmother? He retrieved the

wadded letter and smoothed it out. He may be a tough North Dakota rancher, able to fight wolves, thieves, and rustlers without flinching, but he needed this evidence to prove to his five-foot short granny that his bride had dumped *him* and not the other way around.

Some man he was.

He crossed the dirt street and headed toward the mercantile to place an order. A local rancher, Theodore Roosevelt, strode out of the store and grinned at Quinn.

"Haven't seen you in a while, McFarland. How are things going?"

Quinn shook the man's hand. "Good as can be expected. What brings you to town, Mr. Roosevelt?"

"Call me Theodore." He smiled and shifted the crate of supplies he was holding to his other arm. "I'm staying at my ranch—the Maltese Cross—for a while. Just came into town to get some supplies." The man fingered his bushy moustache. "Sorry to hear about your mother's passing."

"Thank you. It was unexpected." Quinn clenched his jaw. The fever that took his mother two months ago came fast and swift, surprising them all. He didn't want to think about missing her—wondering if he'd done all he could to ease her burden after his pa had died. He gazed down the dirt street that would turn into a muddy mess if the storm clouds dumped the rain they were threatening. He turned his focus back on the rancher. "I haven't been to town in a while. How have things been going around here?"

Theodore slid his hat back on his head. "Heard there was a bank robbery yesterday morning. Most exciting thing that's happened in a long while around here—at least that's what the clerk in the store said. It was unfortunate that the banker's daughter got shot. Seems she had just ridden up to the bank to see her pa when the outlaws came running out. She was shot and fell into the street. Her horse ran off, following the outlaws' horses."

Quinn pursed his lips. "Sorry to hear about that. Do you know how Mary is doing?"

The big man shrugged one shoulder. "Not too good, so the clerk said."

A rider on horseback rode into view, followed by a crowd of people. The rider, a thin boy, looked from side to side as if wondering why so many people were watching him. Quinn wondered the same thing. Normally folks in Medora went about their own business.

He studied the rider and horse. Something was familiar, but he couldn't pinpoint what. Suddenly, he realized what was nagging him. Quinn glanced at Theodore. "That horse looks just like the mare I sold to Mary's pa."

"You don't say. From the way the townsfolk are acting, I would guess it is the same animal."

The murmuring crowd suddenly encircled the horse. The frightened mare tossed her head and whinnied. One man grabbed the reins while another man yanked the rider off the horse. Someone shouted the word "gold." Quinn nodded good-bye to Mr. Roosevelt, stepped off the boardwalk, and moved toward the crowd. What was going on?

Amidst the loud ruckus, the rider was hoisted by each arm and carried toward the sheriff's office. "Hang him," someone shouted, and the crowd roared in agreement.

"Get a rope."

"He needs to pay for what he did to Mary."

Two men deposited the small man on the boardwalk a few feet from the deputy sheriff.

One of them shoved the captive. Stumbling forward, the man flapped his arms like a chicken with clipped wings and fought for balance as he collided with the deputy. His hat flew off, and the crowd instantly hushed as a mass of black hair cascaded down past the man's—no, woman's—shoulders.

Quinn clenched his jaw at the rough way the woman was being manhandled. A skinny man squeezed past her and handed the deputy sheriff a canvas sack. "Look, she's got a bag of gold coins just like the ones that was stolen from our bank."

The deputy eyed his prisoner and his jaw twitched. "You come with me. For your own well-being, I'm locking you up. Sheriff Jones will be back in the morning, and he can straighten out this mess."

The woman dug in her feet. "But I'm innocent. I didn't do anything."

The deputy sheriff shook the heavy bag. "The evidence says otherwise."

two

Quinn shoved his way through the unruly crowd, trying to get closer. The frightened young woman had looked straight at him, their gazes connecting for a split second before hers moved away, as if she was searching for someone to believe her. She was in the deputy's custody, so she was safe from the rowdy crowd for the time being. Had she taken part in yesterday's robbery?

He'd caught the words "stolen gold," but if the woman was guilty of a crime, why would she ride into a town she recently robbed in broad daylight? It had to be some kind of misunderstanding. Sheriff Jones would get to the bottom of it.

A gust of wind threatened to steal Quinn's hat away, and he glanced at the sky. A dust devil swirled at the end of the street, and the air smelled of rain. The clouds had thickened and blocked out the sun that had shone so brightly earlier in the day. He ought to head back to the ranch but didn't want to get caught in a downpour. If he'd been on horseback, he would have toughed it out, but he had the buckboard and wasn't about to drive it in a storm. Not after what happened to his father.

A raindrop tapped against his hat. He hurried his steps and headed toward the general store to place an order for some spices and other supplies his cook and grandmother needed. He'd stay the night in town, and tomorrow morning he'd tend to some business and then ride home.

After checking into his room at the Metropolitan Hotel, he stared out his window watching the heavy raindrops pelt the street. That mail-order bride fiasco had cost him most of a day's work, the cost of the money they sent her, and a hotel stay. His gaze traveled to the jail. He couldn't get that young female outlaw off his mind. Would the sheriff let her go? Was she locked up in the same jail cell Quinn had been confined to after he and his sister had been mistakenly arrested for being outlaws the previous year?

He leaned his head against the cool glass as the darkness of that day crowded in on him. He'd hated that hot, clammy cell that stank like an outhouse. He'd hated not being able to see the sky or feel the warmth of the sun on his skin. Was that what the young woman was now experiencing? If she was guilty of her crimes, she deserved confinement, but if she wasn't. . .

He shook his head and sighed. He had his own problems, mainly being how to keep his grandma from ordering another mail-order bride for him. As soon as he returned home without his bride, the meddling woman would probably start searching the ads. Then again, he could just forget to bring her a newspaper.

Quinn grinned for the first time that day.

☙

"Hey in there! Why won't you listen to me?" Sarah shook the flat bars of the cell that reminded her of wooden lattice, but they held firm. "I'm innocent, I tell you. I didn't rob anyone. I was returning that gold."

She swallowed, her throat raw from yelling so much. She pulled her bodice free from her sweat-dampened chest and fanned it as she paced the tiny, dark cell, her mind racing. Had Ryan and Beth stayed at the shack when she hadn't returned before dark? Had last night's storm frightened them?

A moan escaped her mouth. What if they'd gone back to Uncle Harlan's or attempted to get to town? He could use them as hostages and threaten their lives if she didn't return his gold. Or, what if they were lost in the Badlands?

Tears burned Sarah's eyes, but she refused to let them fall. Had Beth been scared of the storm? Had she awakened this morning and been frightened when she realized her big sister hadn't returned? The little girl had been so fearful that her big sister would be taken away, just like their parents had been, that she'd hardly let Sarah out of sight for the past few months. She shook the black bars of the cell again, but they didn't give.

"God, please, help me. I have to get out of here."

Something skittered across the floor. Sarah jumped back, her heart hammering. A mouse sniffed at something on the dirt floor then dashed under the cot—the cot she'd just spent the night on.

Her thoughts turned back to bigger problems. Why wouldn't that deputy listen to her?

At least the sheriff was due back in town this morning. Maybe he'd be more compassionate and willing to hear her out.

The lock on the entrance to the sheriff's office clicked and the door opened. A tall man with dark hair walked in and stared at Sarah. He leaned against the wall opposite her cell, and his silver badge, which matched his dull gray shirt, reflected in the lantern light.

"I'm Will Jones, Medora's sheriff."

She pressed her face against the slats, glad that he had returned. "I'm innocent. Please, you have to believe me, Sheriff Jones."

The man held up his hand. "I've heard the story."

She *had* to make him believe her. "I was heading into town and found the horse. I rode it to Medora, thinking maybe it had run away from here or one of the area ranches. I didn't steal it. Only rode it so I could get to town and back to my brother and sister sooner. Please, they're little and alone in the hills. Last night's storm probably scared them half to death."

"If they're so helpless, why'd you leave them alone? Why weren't they with you when you came into town?"

Sarah rubbed her palm against her forehead, hoping to chase away her growing headache. "They were exhausted. Beth had twisted her ankle, and she was too heavy for me to carry all the way. I left them in a deserted shack and hurried to town, thinking I'd get back to them before long. Could you at least send someone for them and bring them here?"

The sheriff leaned against the wall and swatted his hand in the air as if batting a fly. "So, the gold was in the saddlebags when you found the horse?"

"What? No. We found it back at my uncle's cabin where we've been staying since our parents died."

"Your uncle? What's his name?"

"Harlan Oakley."

"Never heard of him. Where'd he get the gold?" He lifted one foot and pressed it against the wall behind him.

"My brother, Ryan, overheard our uncle and some men talking about the banks and trains they'd robbed. After Uncle Harlan and the other men rode out yesterday morning, we dug up the gold. I was hoping if I returned it, I might get a reward. I need to get my family away from my uncle and his cronies."

The sheriff pursed his lips, and in two steps, he was at the bars. He grabbed hold of them. Sarah swallowed hard and stepped back.

"So I'm supposed to believe that you already had the gold and then just happened to find a horse that ran away during a robbery the day before. Did you know the woman who owned that horse was shot? The doc doesn't know if she'll pull through. I'm working on getting descriptions of the thieves, but one of them sounds similar in size to you."

"Well, it wasn't me." Sarah grasped the slats of her cell and leaned her forehead against the cold metal. "If you'd just let me go I could show you where I found the horse and take you to my brother and sister. They'll verify my story."

He straightened. "And just how old are these younguns?"

"Beth is six, and Ryan is eight."

"I'd really like to believe your story, ma'am. You seem like a nice young woman, but you were caught red-handed, and you'll have to stay here for now. I'll see that you get some grub in a little while." The sheriff shook his head and turned away.

"*Nooo!* Please listen. I've got to get back to my brother and sister. They've got to be scared and confused, and they don't have much food. If I don't get out of here they could die." Sarah trembled at the thought of all the things that could happen to two unprotected children in the wilds of the Badlands.

Without a backward glance, he shut the door, sealing her in again.

"Don't leave. Wait!" Never had she felt so helpless, not even after the fire that had destroyed her home and killed her parents. "God, why aren't You helping me? We've been through so much already, why this? You know I'm innocent."

The lone lantern cast eerie shadows that danced on the wall across from the two cells. The room smelled of smoke— and the unemptied chamber pot she'd been humiliated to use. If only there was a window to let in fresh air.

A dark panic she'd never before experienced closed in around her. The tears she'd held at bay for so long now flooded down her cheeks. She sat on the cot, elbows on her knees, and a wail escaped, sounding like a panicked animal caught in a trap.

"God, help me. Watch over the kids. Keep them safe, and get me out of here."

Quinn stood outside the hotel, absorbing the warm sunshine. A bird chirped in a nearby tree greeting the new day that smelled fresh and clean after yesterday's storms, but Quinn could hardly enjoy its tune. What would his grandmother say when he returned without his bride? Would she nag him half to death until he found another woman to marry?

He exhaled a frustrated sigh. How could a grown man—a rancher who'd forged a life out of a wilderness—be afraid of his granny? His grandma had always been a strong woman, but mourning her daughter's death had made her frail, and she'd often taken to her bed. A mother shouldn't have to watch her child die, Grandma had said. Now that she was starting to get around again, he didn't want her to have a setback.

He shook his head and crossed the street, dodging a puddle, and headed toward the mercantile. He missed his mother, too, but he had a ranch to run and did his grieving in the saddle. He passed the sheriff's office, and recalled the woman's frantic gaze from the day before—a gaze that had haunted his dreams. Was she still in jail?

It had been a long while since he'd chatted with Sheriff Will Jones. Will had locked up Quinn and his sister when a U.S. Marshal had turned them in as outlaws. After they'd been found innocent and released, he and the sheriff had become friends. Maybe a quick stop to say howdy was in order. Quinn had a burning desire to know what had become of the young woman, and there was only one way to find out. Had she been sent happily on her way, or was she even now incarcerated in that dark, stuffy cell?

He spun around and headed back to the sheriff's office. The door rattled as Quinn stepped inside. Will looked up from the papers on his desk and smiled, weary lines clinging around his eyes. Will gestured toward the chair opposite his desk.

Quinn sat and crossed his arms over his chest. He stretched his legs out in front of him. He still didn't like this place, but at least the office was brighter and less claustrophobic than those two gloomy cells. "Haven't seen you in a coon's age. How you doin'?"

"I've had better days." Will proffered a crooked smile. " 'Course, I've had worse ones, too."

"I imagine you have." Quinn stared at the door separating the office from the cell room. "What became of that gal that your deputy dragged in here yesterday?"

"She's locked up in back." Will rubbed his nape. "I don't know what to believe. She came riding into town on Mary Severson's horse, carrying a bag of stolen gold, and claims she's as innocent as a newborn babe." Will picked up his coffee and took a sip. "The problem is. . .I'm half inclined to believe her. But all the evidence says otherwise."

"It wouldn't be the first time you had an innocent female in your jail."

The sheriff spewed coffee onto the floor and chuckled. "You're never gonna let me live that down. You still mad about that?"

Quinn shook his head. "Nope. It's water under the bridge now. Anna's happily married to that ex-marshal who arrested us. I still can hardly believe that, but Brett's a good man. So, what makes you think this gal is innocent?"

Will scratched his chest, wrinkling his shirt. "Just a hunch. There are no eyewitnesses that can place her at the crime." Will glanced at the closed door to the cell room. "She claims she has a brother and sister out there somewhere waiting for her to return."

Quinn bent his legs and leaned forward. "You think she's telling the truth?"

The sheriff shrugged. "I sent my deputy out to look for them, but he didn't find any trace of two children."

Quinn stared out the window. The sun shone bright on the two small trees across the street, and a light wind tickled leaves still damp from last night's storm. He hated the thought of an innocent woman in that cell, unable to see the sun or feel a breeze on her face, experiencing the same fears his sister had endured until he, too, had been arrested. But maybe the woman *was* guilty. How else could she have had stolen gold in her possession?

Will leaned forward and laid his arms across his desk. "I have a bad feeling about this one. The townsfolk were ready to lynch her yesterday. The odd thing is that bank bag she had in her possession had the name of the Deadwood Federal Bank on it. I telegraphed the Deadwood sheriff, and they had a robbery over a month ago, but there wasn't a woman involved."

Loud footsteps pounded on the boardwalk, and a heavy-set man dressed in a three-piece brown suit strode past the window. He halted in front of the sheriff's door.

"Great. Here comes trouble." Will leaned back in his chair and crossed his arms.

The man flung open the door and stormed inside. He glanced at Quinn and then focused a glare on the sheriff. Quinn recognized Medora's bank president, Lars Severson. The wealthy white-haired man had often tried to push his own agenda at town meetings.

Sweat trickled down Severson's temple. He marched forward, put his hands on the desk, and leaned toward the sheriff. "I want to know what you plan to do with that outlaw who shot Mary and stole her horse."

Will stood, forcing Mr. Severson to look up. "I haven't decided yet. Witnesses have testified that Mary's horse ran off riderless following the outlaws' horses, but a few folks say one of the outlaws was on it."

"My Mary lies half dead in her bed, and you can't decide

what to do with the outlaw who shot her?" The man's beefy face turned the color of a beet. He pounded his fist on the sheriff's desk, rattling an empty coffee cup. "I demand justice."

Will shoved his hands to his waist and stood. "Now see here, there's no proof this woman was with the outlaws who shot Mary. She claims she found the horse and the gold. . . but not at the same place." Will glanced at Quinn as if the story sounded highly unlikely once voiced out loud.

"I want that woman to pay for her crimes."

"You want to send an innocent woman to prison or see her hanged?" Will asked.

The banker's white brows crinkled. "Of course not, but there's plenty of evidence that the woman in your jail is a thief."

"Nobody has stepped forward who can identify her as one of the outlaws, and there was no mention of a woman being among the gang of robbers. I'm not convinced she was." The sheriff stared at the banker until the man looked away.

A distant memory clawed its way to the front of Quinn's mind. "I can think of a way to get rid of this headache." Both men swung their gaze on him, and he struggled to keep a straight face. Maybe he could defuse the tension with a bit of jesting.

"How?" Will asked. "I'm open to any ideas at this point."

"I remember reading in the newspaper about a woman outlaw who was captured in Montana. Since there were so few women around those parts, the sheriff auctioned her off to the highest bidder."

Will stared at him. "You're joking, right?"

"Nope." He may have been joking about auctioning off the woman in Will's jail, but the tale he told was true. "That sheriff didn't want the hassle of keeping a woman in his jail until a judge rode through."

"That's preposterous, Sheriff." Banker Severson looked from Quinn to the sheriff. "Surely you aren't taking him seriously, are you?"

Quinn shrugged. "I'm just telling you what another sheriff did in a similar situation. But you've got to admit there are few women around these parts. Do you really think a jury made up of men from around here would convict a pretty gal?"

Will seemed to consider that. "Probably not."

"Why not give her the choice of marrying now and getting out of jail or trying her luck at a jury trial? That way if she is innocent, she won't pay for a crime she didn't do, and the jail will be free for more serious criminals."

"Why. . .that's unseemly—unchristian," the banker sputtered. "What could be more serious than shooting an innocent girl and robbing a bank?"

Will gave Quinn a furtive wink and rubbed his jaw and glanced toward the closed door that led to the cell area. "That's not a half bad idea. Women *are* hard to come by in these parts."

The banker pounded his fist on Will's desk again. "I demand justice. That woman must account for her misdeeds." Mr. Severson glared at them then turned and stomped out the door.

Quinn chuckled. "He just might have your job for that."

"It was worth it. Did you see the look on his face?" Will hooted and pounded on his desk. "That man has been a thorn in my side ever since he came to town. I'm real sorry Mary got shot, but I'd rather lose my job than send an innocent woman to prison or see her hanged."

Will walked to the window and stared out. "Uh oh, looks like Severson is making a stink already. Half a dozen men are headed this way."

Quinn stood and joined him at the window. Sure enough, they were about to be swarmed. Will spun around, grabbed his rifle, and pulled a box of cartridges out of his top desk drawer, preparing for a fight. Quinn checked his revolver out of habit, knowing already that it was loaded. "We can't let them lynch that woman."

Will nodded. "It's days like this I wish the jail had a back door."

three

Quinn cocked his gun and watched the growing crowd. Half a dozen men shouted and shoved at one another as if each wanted to be the one to pull the trap door and lynch that poor girl. Will opened the door and stood there, blocking the entrance.

"Just stop right where you are, or someone's gonna get hurt."

The men at the front of the crowd halted, surprise lifting their brows. Men in the back plowed into them. More pushing and caterwauling ensued.

Tom Gallagher, a local rancher, shoved past another man and stepped forward. "I'll marry that gal. It don't matter to me what she's done. She's right fair to look at, and I need a woman at home."

A smelly, hairy man who resembled a bear fresh out of hibernation stepped in front of Mr. Gallagher. "Nuh-uh, I's here first. Heard Lars Severson myself say the sheriff was marryin' her off. She's my woman."

Pete Samson wiped his sleeve across his whiskery face. "Nope." He spat a wad of tobacco juice at Will's feet. "I reckon I was first. She's mine."

Will's confused gaze darted to Quinn's, and he shrugged one shoulder.

"What are you talking about?" Will asked. "I thought you were a lynch mob."

The bear tugged off his dingy cap. "Nope. That was yesterday. Today, I reckon we all got our hearts set on marryin' that little gal—and I'm first in line."

"No you're not," Tom Gallagher hollered. "I need a wife to watch after my two younguns. You just want her for, well. . . never mind."

"It don't matter why I want her. I just do." The two men shoved at each other like schoolboys wanting to do a favor for a pretty teacher.

Pete stared at the two, then grinned and stepped past them. "Reckon I'm first now, Sheriff."

Several men still standing on the boardwalk yelled that they wanted to marry up with the outlaw, too. One man punched another, and a jaw-breaking brawl started. Sheriff Jones pointed his rifle over their heads and pulled the trigger. The blast of the gunfire froze the crowd as the familiar odor of gunpowder scented the air in a cloud of smoke. Men with fists raised slowly lowered their arms and glared at their neighbor.

"Nothing has been decided yet. Go home." Will held his rifle across one arm.

"But Banker Severson was griping to anyone who'd listen. Said you was gonna auction that gal off. I'll give ya two dollars for her." A man Quinn had never seen before jingled some coins in his hand.

Will growled. "We don't sell people around here. Go home before I lock up the whole kit and caboodle of you."

"If'n you're gonna lock me up with that gal, then go ahead." The bear held out his hands as if waiting for Will to slap irons on him. Several men chuckled.

Will aimed his rifle at the man's belly. "You just head back to the hills, mister."

Irritation sparked in the man's eyes, but his gaze lowered to the rifle. He backed away, mumbling something Quinn couldn't make out, and sauntered across the street.

Quinn bit back a chuckle. Yesterday they were ready to lynch the poor gal and now they wanted to marry her. The crowd of fickle men had been disappointed. That was obvious. Twenty men to one woman. No wonder they all went half crazy for a chance to have one of their own. His mail-order bride's refusal stung again. Yep, it sure would be hard to find a woman to live on a ranch, two hours' ride from town.

Will shook his head and remained just outside the doorway. "Look what you started."

Quinn shrugged. "Men out here are lonely. I was only trying to help." He leaned one shoulder against the doorframe. "But you can't turn that poor girl over to the likes of any of those men. Gallagher's not so bad. He needs a woman for those kids of his, but he's got that hair-trigger temper and those rambunctious boys."

Will rubbed the back of his neck. "I wouldn't let that poor gal marry a one of those hooligans."

"Well. . .why not find a man you *would* let her marry—if you're sure of her innocence."

Will's eyes sparked and one corner of his mouth tilted up. He stepped back into his office and laid his rifle on the desk. "I think I will. How'd you like to meet your new bride, McFarland?"

"What?" Quinn scowled at Will. "That's not funny."

Will placed his hands on his desk and leaned toward Quinn. "Do I look like I'm joking? That little gal is as pretty as a mustang. I feel in my gut that she's telling the truth. You need a wife, so why not marry her? Would solve a lot of problems—for both of us."

Quinn turned to leave. "That's just plain crazy, Will. You don't even know if she'd be willing to marry just to get out of jail." He walked to the open door and noted that the crowd of men outside had grown to more than a dozen. Most weren't family men who worked hard and made a good living, but rather the bums, trappers, and cowpokes that hung out at the saloon. It didn't take much thought to realize why they wanted a woman.

"She seems willing to do just about anything to get out of jail. Think about it, will you?"

Coming home with a bride *would* solve one of his problems. It would get Grandma off his back, so he could focus on his work. He turned to face the sheriff.

"Did you see her yesterday?" Will's eyes brightened. "She's a comely little thing. You want to have a look up close before you decide?"

Quinn clenched his teeth and scowled. Will made it sound as if he were buying a horse. But his curiosity had been aroused. He wasn't one to make impulsive decisions, especially when an outlaw was part of the deal, but what did it hurt to look at the woman?

Muffled cries came from the back room where the woman was jailed. Quinn stared at the door that led to the cells. Was the woman as frightened as Anna had been in there? "I'd like to see her." The words came out before he could lasso them back.

Will stared at him for a moment then grinned. "She'll give you an earful. She's a feisty little thing."

Quinn wished he'd kept his mouth shut. He needed to get his supplies and head home. But he wasn't in any hurry to disappoint his grandmother.

"I need to talk to her anyway. C'mon." Will stood and shuffled across the room, digging a key from his pocket. The latch clicked, and he opened the door.

That sound was enough to make Quinn sweat. The feeling of being totally helpless—of knowing he was innocent but no one believed him—hit him full force in the chest. For a moment, he wasn't sure he could walk through that door again.

"You comin'?" Will called as he peered around the doorway. He grinned. "Got cold feet, McFarland?"

Quinn narrowed his eyes at the man and sucked in a breath. He strode to the door and halted. The dank odor of mold and a chamber pot assailed him. He'd never been afraid of anything except losing his good reputation when he had been locked up for a crime he hadn't committed. Quinn stepped halfway across the threshold. He could see plenty well from there.

Will chuckled and faced the prisoner. The memory of Anna alone in the cell before Quinn had been arrested hit him suddenly as his gaze landed on the red-faced waif. Why, the girl couldn't be out of her teens yet. Quinn's irritation with Will grew. Wasn't imprisoning one woman enough for him?

She wiped her eyes and hiked up her chin as her confused gaze darted between Quinn and Will. She grabbed the bars, and her gaze turned frantic. "Please, I'm innocent. You've got to believe me."

Bile rose to Quinn's throat. She wasn't a hard-edged criminal, but a frightened young woman. Her haunted eyes held desperate fear, not the cold, hardened guilt of an outlaw. She was as innocent as Anna had been. He knew it in his gut.

Will shook his head. "I want to believe you, miss, but there's the gold and horse you had in your possession. Horse stealing is a hangin' offense in these parts."

"But I didn't steal it. I found it, and I was returning the gold. It didn't come from Medora. You can clearly see that if you look at the bag it was in." Her gaze darted to Quinn as if he could help her.

"You need anything, miss? More water?" Will asked.

She glared at him. "I just need to get out. Ryan and Beth are depending on me."

Will heaved a heavy sigh and nodded for Quinn to head back into the office. Quinn was glad to be away from that dark hole. The door clanked as Will pulled it shut, sending a shiver down Quinn's spine.

"Now you see why I can't marry her off to just anyone—if I decide to go that route. She's too young and naive."

"You don't even know if she'd want to marry. She's just a kid." Quinn leaned against the wall across from Will's desk. He glanced at the locked door, glad he was on this side of it.

"She said something about her parents dying." Will leaned back in his chair and propped his feet onto his desk.

Quinn stared out the window, knowing the pain of losing one's parents. He needed to get going. Grandma would be fit to be tied that he hadn't come home yesterday. Too bad he didn't have a good enough excuse to stay gone another week.

"What are you grinning about? I don't see anything funny." Will laced his hands behind his head and leaned back in his chair.

Quinn stared at the wanted poster above Will's head. He was glad the girl's pretty face wasn't up there. Her eyes had looked like yesterday's storm clouds one moment and then turned soft and sincere. . .pleading, the next. Her long, dark hair reminded him of a wild mustang when she'd flipped it over her shoulder.

"I said, what's so funny?"

Quinn took a deep breath and told his friend what his grandma had done. Will's eyes went wide.

"That's not the worst part. The bride didn't come. Wrote me a letter saying she'd changed her mind."

Will slapped his leg and hooted with laughter. "Dumped by a bride you didn't even want. Oh, that's a good one."

Quinn straightened. "Don't you tell anyone. A man's got his pride, you know."

"Are you threatening a lawman?" Will grinned wickedly, then suddenly sobered. Quinn glanced out the window to see if something had drawn his attention.

"So"—Will's feet dropped to the floor and he leaned forward—"let me get this straight. Your grandma ordered you a bride who didn't show. Now you've got to go home and tell her. No wonder you've been dawdling in my office so long."

"I'm not dawdling. I'm paying a friendly visit." Quinn picked up his hat from Will's desk. "I can see I've worn out my welcome."

"Hold on. I can help."

"How?"

Will grinned again. "I've got a gal in my jail who needs a husband."

Quinn narrowed his eyes. Suddenly he realized what Will meant. "Oh, no. You're not going to pawn her off onto me. I never said I'd marry her. I just wanted a look at her."

"Hold on." Will held up his calloused hand. "Let's think this through. You need a bride—"

"No. I don't." Quinn rolled his eyes. He didn't need a bride, especially an outlaw one, although Anna would love that story.

"I saw how that gal affected you. She's frightened and alone, just like your sister was when she was locked up before you were. I've got a feeling she's innocent. A good man like you could keep a woman on the straight and narrow."

Quinn's gaze darted to the closed door. Anna had been so scared and heartbroken to be locked up in jail. He felt sure the woman was innocent, but what if she wasn't?

"You said yourself that women are hard to come by out here. You'd better take the bird-in-the-hand."

"Don't you mean bird-in-the-cell?" Quinn cocked a brow.

Will shrugged. "You want to marry her or not? I've got plenty of others ready to jump at the chance."

Quinn gritted his teeth. He didn't like being coerced into doing something but couldn't get that tear-streaked face out of his mind. That gal had looked scared to death—and innocent. If she was guilty, she wouldn't be putting up such a ruckus, and the thought of one of those mangy men getting their hands on someone so naive stuck in his craw. "How do you even know she'd want to marry me? I have to be ten years her senior."

Will waved his hand in the air. "That doesn't matter. Herbert Simms is fifteen years older than his wife. You'd be doing me a huge favor, Quinn. How can I arrest real criminals if I have a woman in my jail? I couldn't subject her to that."

The girl was comely enough, and if he married her, one of his problems would be solved. Quinn grinned. "It would almost be worth it to see Grandma's face. She's expecting a hazel-eyed redhead."

"Wish I could be there to see her reaction. But this ain't no laughing matter. Marriage is for life. So. . .you willing?"

Quinn swallowed, unable to believe he could actually go through with such a crazy plan. He wasn't one to be impulsive. He preferred to think through things and look at them from all angles. He couldn't explain why, but he felt marrying this woman was the right thing to do. Swallowing hard, he nodded. "I'm willing. . .if she is."

❧

The outer door opened again, and Sarah jumped off the cot, hit by a wave of dizziness. The lack of sleep and appetite, along with the stagnant air and worry for her siblings had left her woozy. She held on to the bars as the sheriff and his friend entered again. The other man was taller than the sheriff with shoulders so wide he looked uncomfortable in the narrow walkway. His brown hair matched his dark eyes, which held a mixture of curiosity and apprehension. He twisted his western hat in his hands.

He leaned against the doorjamb, with one foot barely over the threshold, as if he were afraid to come in further. He glanced over his shoulder. Perhaps he didn't like small, confining spaces. Well. . .neither did she.

The sheriff stopped in front of her and stared as if taking

her measure. She'd just finished braiding her hair and tying it off with a piece of fabric she'd torn from the tail of her shirt.

Sheriff Jones cleared his throat. "You say you're innocent, Miss Oakley, and I'm inclined to believe you. The law out here is—shall we say—a bit more flexible than back East, and there are times a sheriff has to go with his gut, and mine says you're not guilty."

Sarah's heart jumped. Was he going to release her?

He rubbed his hand over his cheek. "I have a proposal for you, miss. Well. . .I don't but he does." The sheriff used his thumb to point at the stranger, and his lips tugged up in a cocky grin.

Sarah narrowed her gaze and glanced at the tall man. How could he help her?

Sheriff Jones cleared his voice. "Here's the thing, ma'am. I got nobody who can identify you as the thief who shot Mary and stole her horse."

Sarah hiked up her chin. "That's because I didn't do it."

"Be that as it may, here's the deal. You can sit in this cell until the circuit judge from Dickinson comes around in a month or so, or. . ." The sheriff glanced at the other man, who looked at Sarah then pursed his lips and nodded.

Her heart thundered and her knees shook. No matter what the alternative was, she had to take it.

"Or you can marry up with this man and get out of jail today."

Sarah's mouth dipped down, but no words came out. Surely the sheriff couldn't be serious. Marry a stranger?

She glanced at the other man—the one who was willing to marry her. Why would he want to wed a woman he didn't know? A woman in jail, no less. He was handsome enough to marry any woman he wanted. She looked him in the eye and swallowed back her fear. He was the key to getting out of here. "Why?"

He glanced at the sheriff and twisted the hat in his hand. The lantern cast flickering light across his face. "Why what?"

"Why would you want to marry me?"

He studied his hat for a moment. With his head ducked down, Sarah saw that his hair had a curl to it. "I've got my reasons."

"There's no point in you wasting away in jail when you can marry Quinn. He owns one of the best ranches in this area. He's got, what"—the sheriff glanced sideways—"a couple of thousand acres?"

"Four thousand."

"And he's got one of the finest cabins I've seen. He's an honorable man and raises some of the best cattle and horses in these parts."

Sarah's mind raced but nothing made sense. She looked at the sheriff. "You're saying if I agree to marry him"—she pointed at the stranger—"then I can go free? Today? I wouldn't have to come back to stand trial?"

Sheriff Jones nodded. "Yep. I don't much like having a woman locked up in my jail. Causes all kinds of problems. I figure if you marry up with Quinn, he'll keep you out of trouble and my jail will be free for real outlaws."

"Does *he* have a last name?"

"McFarland," the sheriff and her potential husband said at the same time. The sheriff chuckled, but Mr. McFarland scowled.

At least he understood this wasn't a laughing matter. "I do have one question," her would-be spouse said, as he stared her in the eye.

Sarah swallowed the lump in her throat and resisted the urge to flee to the back of the cell. He looked fierce enough to make a person do what he wanted. Would he be mean to her if she married him? To Ryan and Beth?

"I have an ailing grandmother. She's got her mind set on

finding me a bride before she dies. If I marry up with you, will you treat her kindly? Take care of her while I'm out working the ranch?"

Ahhh. . .so that was it. Sarah nodded and clung to the slats of the cell, relieved that what he asked was something she could easily agree to. "Yes, I'd be happy to care for your grandmother—if I decide to marry you. Mine died before I was born and I've always wanted one."

Mr. McFarland visibly relaxed and nodded his gratitude. Sarah licked her lips. Maybe she was pushing her luck, but she had to know. "Are you a God-fearing man, Mr. McFarland?"

He blinked then glanced sideways. The sheriff grinned. A muscle ticked in Mr. McFarland's clean-shaven jaw. "I believe in the good Lord, ma'am. It's just that He and I aren't as close as we should be."

Was any person ever as close to God as they could be? His answer wasn't what she'd hoped for, but it would suffice. "You wouldn't ever hit a woman or child, would you?"

His expression, which had just softened, turned hard. His dark eyes glinted. "I resent that question."

The sheriff turned to him. "Now, Quinn, it's a fair question. She don't know you, and she's considering becoming your wife."

"Of course I wouldn't. What decent man would?" Mr. McFarland crossed his arms, pulling his shirt tight across his wide shoulders.

Sarah's mouth went dry. If he treated her as nice as he looked, she'd be all right, but she knew that handsome men could be as hurtful as ugly ones. Hadn't her uncle proven that?

"Do you like children?"

The sheriff snorted and seemed to be holding in his laughter. He looked at Mr. McFarland with his brows raised. "You want kids, Quinn?"

Mr. McFarland's eyes widened. "Well. . .I hardly think this is the place to discuss such a matter."

Oh, dear. They had misconstrued her inquiry. Sarah was grateful for the dimness of the room. She hadn't considered how he'd take that question. She opened her mouth to explain but slammed it shut. He was her only way out of this cell. If he knew she had two siblings, he might rescind his offer. If he misunderstood, so be it.

She wasn't sure but thought he might be blushing. "So. . . do you like children?"

He straightened. "I reckon I like them as much as any man. I've got the cutest nephew in the world." A soft grin tilted his lips.

"I guess we ought to give the gal some time to think about your proposal, Quinn." The sheriff nudged his chin toward his office, indicating Quinn should head out of the cell room.

He nodded at her. With her whole being trembling, Sarah watched him turn, slow and easy. So in control of his big body. She had no real choice. She had to get out of jail and get back to Ryan and Beth. This Quinn McFarland was her only option. She'd hoped to marry for love like her parents had, but that wasn't to be. According to the sheriff, this man had a nice home and a good ranch. Ryan and Beth would have plenty of food to eat and a decent place to stay.

But was it far enough away that Uncle Harlan couldn't find them?

Would they be safe on an isolated ranch?

The sheriff reached out to close the door.

"Wait. I—I'll marry him."

four

"Will you take this man to be your lawfully wedded husband, ma'am?"

Sarah stared at the skinny parson who waited with lifted brows, a worn Bible tucked against his chest. Was this truly what she wanted?

Dodging his stare, she let her gaze skip past the sheriff, and she peered around his sparse office, so unlike a church, where she'd always wanted to be married. Instead of stained glass windows, there were dingy panes looking out on a muddy street. Instead of her family to celebrate what should be the most joyous of days, stern-faced outlaws glared at her from the wanted posters on the walls.

Mr. McFarland peered down at her, looking as if he'd swallowed a wormy apple. Could she actually marry this stranger? Was he having second thoughts, too? He may have another option, but she didn't. She nodded, before he could change his mind.

"You'll have to say the words out loud, miss." The parson rubbed a finger along his thin moustache. He looked more like a gambler than a minister.

She hated marrying a man she didn't know, but he was her only chance to get out of jail. Sarah cleared her throat. "Yes, I will take him as my husband."

The parson nodded. "All right then, I reckon you two are hitched." He glanced at Mr. McFarland and grinned. "You can kiss your bride now, Quinn."

Heat engulfed her cheeks. Sarah could feel the warmth emanating off her husband's—oh, that word was hard to swallow—arm as he stood beside her, not moving an inch. The back of his hand had bumped hers during the brief ceremony, and he'd jerked away. He didn't want to touch, much less kiss her.

"I reckon we can skip that part, Parson. We've a long ride ahead and need to get on the road." Mr. McFarland shoved his hat on his head and handed the man some coins from his pocket.

Skipping the kissing part was the right thing to do since this wasn't a love union. So why was she disappointed that he felt the same way? They were united together for life. Was it foolish to hope he might grow to like her one day?

In the light of the office window, Sarah realized her husband's hair was a dark blond and not plain brown as she'd thought earlier, and his eyes were such a deep brown that she could barely make out his pupils. He had nice eyes, when they weren't glaring.

"You ready?" He caught her watching him.

She turned to the sheriff. "Am I free to go?"

He nodded. "Yes, Mrs. McFarland. You sure are. I'll escort you two until you're clear of town, just so you don't have problems with anyone."

"I'm obliged, Will." Her husband spun toward the door. He strode outside, then turned back quickly and held the door open for her.

Sarah forced a smile and walked outside, blinking against the sun she hadn't seen in nearly a day. Her stomach gurgled. She was hungry but anxious to be on their way. *Please, God, let Beth and Ryan be where I left them.*

"I've got to pick up my buckboard from the livery and get supplies at the mercantile; then we can head out." He glanced down at Sarah's pants and grimaced. "You got any clothes besides those?"

She knew how bad she looked in her uncle's baggy

clothing, especially after being locked up in that grimy cell. She could do with a bath, but she didn't want to take the time, not that he'd given her that option. "I have a dress back where I left my belongings."

"Just one?" He pursed his lips.

Sarah nodded. She'd had another one, but she could hardly tell him that she'd cut it down to make Beth a dress. Her husband turned and walked away. Sarah stood where she was, watching the townsfolk watching her. A few people gathered outside a building across the street, glaring at her. A man riding a horse stopped in the middle of the road and stared. Sarah wiped her sweaty hands on her pants, and peered over her shoulder at the sheriff, who stood a few feet away. Were these people still bent on lynching her?

Mr. McFarland glanced back, spun around, and stalked toward her. She flinched as he stopped in front of her. Had she upset him already? He studied her and then scanned the crowd of townsfolk. He offered her his arm. "May I assist you, ma'am?"

Grateful for the protection he offered, Sarah looped her hand around his arm. It was rock hard, and her hand shook at his overpowering nearness. The sheriff walked on her right side, and she felt cocooned between them. Other than her pa, she'd never had a man stand up for her. This was something she could easily get used to. She alone had borne the burden these past months of finding shelter and food and caring for her siblings after their farmhouse had burned with their parents inside. It was nice to have someone watching out for *her* again.

They walked into the mercantile and all talk stopped. Her husband strode to the counter, all but dragging her along. "Are my supplies ready to go?"

The plump, white-haired woman behind the counter nodded her head and looked Sarah up and down. Mr.

McFarland's jaw tightened. He turned to Sarah. "I want you to pick out a new dress, and some fabric to make several more." His eyes narrowed. "You *can* sew, can't you?"

Sarah nodded, grateful for his generosity but anxious to be on her way. She needed to know her brother and sister were all right. He leaned toward her. "Be sure to get any, uh"—he leaned closer, his warm breath tickling her ear—"unmentionables that you might need. We don't get to town all that often."

He stepped away, his ears and neck as red as she was sure her cheeks were, and looked back at the clerk. "Make sure she gets a sturdy pair of shoes, too. I'm going to fetch my wagon. I want her ready to go when I get back." He strode out of the store without a backward glance.

"I'll just rest here while you shop." The sheriff smiled and leaned his hip against the countertop.

The clerk nodded, but Quinn was already gone. Sarah was sure he didn't often shop for ladies' clothing and couldn't help grinning at his embarrassment.

The sheriff chuckled. "Quinn lit out of here like his britches was on fire. What a day he's had. First he gets married, then he has to buy a lady's unmentionables."

The clerk twisted her mouth. "Maybe such unmentionables should remain unmentioned, Sheriff."

Will Jones grinned. "Maybe so, ma'am. I'll just stay here by the counter while you two do the shopping."

Sarah looked around the store. It was smaller than the ones she'd been in before, but most everything anyone would need was crammed on a shelf or cabinet or stuffed in a corner.

"I don't know where to start." She'd never been able to buy whatever she wanted before. Her parents' farm had provided most of the things her family had needed, and they had traded for other necessities. A man and woman to her left eyed Sarah with speculation, the man whispered something, and then they hurried out the door.

"Our ready-made dresses are in the back. We don't have too many since most folks in these parts make their own." The clerk didn't seem fazed in the least that her customer had just gotten out of jail. She was probably counting up the big sale she was about to make.

Sarah held her breath as she looked at the four dresses hanging on a narrow rod—one blue, one dark green, and two brown calicos. She'd never had a store-bought dress before. She loved green and reached out to touch the garment but then looked down at her dirty palm. Her hand dropped to her side. Tears blurred her view of the dresses. After all she'd been through, why should something so small make her cry?

"You know, I've got a room in back where you could freshen up if you've a mind to."

Sarah smiled at the woman's gracious offer. "That would be wonderful. Thank you."

She followed the clerk to the back of the store. As they walked toward a curtain separating the store from another room, the sheriff pushed off the counter and strode toward her.

The clerk sashayed around Sarah and stopped in front of her, crossing her arms over her ample chest. "Now, Sheriff, the lady would like to freshen up. Surely you can't deny her that after all she's been through."

Sheriff Jones studied both women as if he thought they were up to something.

"I'm not going anywhere. I just want to get this layer of grime off me. Please." Sarah begged with her eyes for him to grant her this one little favor.

He flung the curtain aside and glanced at the store's closed back door that she'd have access to once the curtain was shut again. Finally, he nodded. "Just don't forget there's a town full of men out there who were ready to lynch you yesterday." He strode back toward the counter. "Or marry you."

Had she heard correctly? She shook her head. Surely there hadn't been more than one man willing to marry her.

The clerk slid the floral curtain shut, blocking Sarah's view of the sheriff. A colorful ceramic pitcher with painted flowers sat in a matching basin on a worktable next to the wall. The older woman poured water into the basin and laid a washcloth and a bar of scented soap on the table.

"This is a special soap. I only carry a few bars, but I want you to have it."

Sarah batted back tears. After being jailed, this small kindness just about destroyed her composure. "Thank you so much."

"I'm sure you deserve it. I don't know what this world is coming to when they put girls in jail. No sir." She shook her head. "Now go ahead and strip down. I'll get some fresh under things and that green dress you were eyeing. It might be a tad long, but you can hem it once you get a chance. My man is gone on a delivery and won't be back until this afternoon, so no one will bother you back here. I'm Mrs. Johnson, by the way."

She dashed away before Sarah could utter another thank-you. The scent of leather mixed with the odor of spices, pickles, and coffee made her stomach rumble. An abundance of canned items were stocked on shelves that went all the way up to the ceiling of the storage room. It looked as if Mrs. Johnson had already stocked up for winter, even though it was still months away.

Sarah wiped away the grime that had collected over the past two days. She slipped out of her uncle's smelly clothes, grateful to be rid of them. They'd make good fuel for someone's fire.

Standing in her frayed undergarments, Sarah flinched when the curtain moved, and she stepped back beside a cabinet, lest the sheriff see her. Mrs. Johnson slipped through the curtain, taking care to keep it closed around her. "Here you go."

On her arm were stockings, a chemise and drawers with eyelet trim, and a pretty petticoat. Sarah reached out and rubbed the soft cotton fabric between her fingers. The unmentionables she and her mother had made were from rough flour sacks. "I've never had anything so beautiful."

Mrs Johnson smiled congenially. "Most men won't say so, but they love seeing their woman in pretty things."

Sarah's eyes widened at the thought of Mr. McFarland seeing her half dressed. "I suppose I'd better hurry. My. . .uh. . . husband will be back any minute."

Mrs. Johnson chuckled as she laid the green dress on a chair. "I'll gather up another three sets of undergarments for you, if that's all right. Two for warm weather and two for when it gets colder."

"Don't you think that's too much? One or two would be sufficient."

"We have some long winters here, and it's hard for the ranchers to get to town. It's better that you have too much than too little."

Sarah shrugged. "I suppose you're right."

Mrs. Johnson slipped around the floral curtain again. Sarah dressed quickly, enjoying the feel of the fresh cotton dress and soft undergarments. She could only hope her husband wouldn't be angry at her for buying so many things. But he did say to get whatever she needed.

She smoothed down her dress, wishing it didn't drag on the floor. She picked up the front of her skirt and peeked around the curtain for Mrs. Johnson. Sheriff Jones craned his neck as if checking to see if she was still there. She couldn't resist waving. He shook his head, and a grin tugged at one corner of his mouth.

"Try these on. I think they're your size."

Sarah stared at the lovely boots Mrs. Johnson passed to her. The soft black leather was cool to the touch. "I can't buy these. They're too much." Reluctantly, she handed them back.

"Nonsense. Your husband said to get you a sturdy pair, and these are the best we've got. Go ahead and try them on."

Sarah sighed and slipped on the new boots. They fit as if they were made for her.

"You look lovely, my dear. Let me do something with your hair. I'm sure you'd like to wash it, but this cornmeal will have to do for now." She sprinkled on some cornmeal and brushed it through Sarah's tresses. In a manner of minutes, Mrs. Johnson had coiled Sarah's hair and pinned it up. The woman handed her a mirror. "Have a look."

Sarah held it up, staring at herself. Melancholy battled with delight. Not since before her parents died had she looked so nice. If only her mother could see her. Would she be angered at how Sarah had left her brother and sister alone? Or would she be proud of Sarah's efforts to keep the children together?

"That husband of yours won't know what hit him when he sees how lovely you are."

Sarah smiled and checked the mirror again. Would Quinn think she was pretty?

"Now, let's hurry and pick out some fabric before your Mr. McFarland returns. He seemed anxious to be on his way."

The sheriff's brows lifted and a low whistle escaped his lips. "Wow. If I'd have known you'd clean up so well, I'd have married you myself."

Heat rushed to Sarah's cheeks. "Why, Sheriff, I do believe that was a compliment."

The rogue grinned and pushed his hat back on his forehead as if to get a better look.

Ten minutes later, Sarah had enough fabric to make two more dresses, as well as clothes and undergarments for both Ryan and Beth. She added a brush and comb and some hair ribbons to the pile. She wished she could get new shoes for her siblings, but how could she explain that? She hoped Mr. McFarland wouldn't question why she'd purchased so much fabric, because she wasn't ready to let the cat out of the bag quite yet.

Boots clomped on the boardwalk, and Sarah spun around to face her husband. He stopped a few feet into the doorway. His gaze moved past her then rushed back. His mouth dropped open. Quickly enough, he slammed it shut, but his gaze traveled her length from head to toe. A slow smile tugged at his lips. "Well. . .that's an improvement."

Sarah pressed her hands against her chest, embarrassed at his perusal. She'd never had a man look as if he was so pleased with her appearance. "I was hoping that you meant for me to wear the store-bought dress so that I'd look nicer when I meet your grandmother."

"Honestly, I just didn't want you to have to wear those filthy duds any longer."

"More likely, he didn't want to have to smell them all the way to the Rocking M." The sheriff grinned.

Mrs. Johnson gasped, grabbed a nearby broom, and swatted the sheriff's boots. "What an awful thing to say. You ought to be ashamed of yourself, Will Jones."

Chuckling, the sheriff danced out of her way. He grabbed the two large packages that Mrs. Johnson had wrapped in brown paper and hurried out of the store with the clerk at his heels. Mr. McFarland pulled some paper dollars from his pocket and paid the woman when she returned. He glanced at Sarah with one brow lifted when the woman quoted the exorbitant total. Sarah tried to soothe herself with the thought that her husband had purchased several crates of supplies himself, too, but it wasn't working. She cringed at the thought of spending so much of his money and for deceiving him about the children. But would he have married her if he'd known about Ryan and Beth ahead of time?

"Ready to go?"

Sarah avoided his gaze and nodded. The sheriff might have been joking about how she smelled, but what he'd said was true. She'd cleaned up some and the rose-scented soap helped, but she still needed a bath.

Mr. McFarland took her elbow and steered her toward the door. "Don't let what Will said bother you. You can have all the baths you want when we get home. I've been in that jail before, so I know what it's like."

She peeked up at him. Why in the world had he been in jail? Was that why he'd been so willing to marry her?

He lifted her up onto a solid buckboard with a padded seat and back rest. "Are you all set? Did you get everything you needed?"

"Yes. That was very generous of you to allow me to purchase so many things. Thank you." Sarah was grateful that Sheriff Jones's comment had distracted her husband from the large packages that the sheriff had set among the crates of supplies he helped load.

Mr. McFarland grunted a response as if uncomfortable with her gratitude. The wagon swayed as he climbed in. His big body took up much of the bench. Sarah scooted to the right, bumping the edge of the seat.

He clicked to the horses, and they started forward. The townsfolk gathered on the boardwalk, a few waving, but most grumbling and glaring. Mr. McFarland and the sheriff had spoiled their lynching. Sarah reached up, her hand touching her throat.

Her husband turned the wagon in the opposite direction of the Little Missouri River and the big smokestack that had guided her to town. Away from Ryan and Beth.

five

Quinn slapped the reins on the horses' rumps, and they walked faster. He rubbed the back of his neck, as he considered how he'd explain Sarah to his grandmother.

"No, wait." Sarah clutched Quinn's arm, and he looked down.

"What's wrong?"

"I need to go the other way—to collect my belongings."

"I just bought you two parcels of things. I thought you realized that I purchased those items so you wouldn't have to return for your other dress." Was that so hard to understand? He needed to get home. Work was waiting. He couldn't be traveling all over the Badlands to pick up an old dress.

Sarah sputtered then glared at him. "There are other things I need besides my dress."

"Can't you get them at the store?"

"Um. . .no, I can't. They're things especially dear to me. All I have left of my parents."

Quinn stared out the corner of his eye at her then sighed. Pulling tight on the left rein, he turned the buckboard in a wide arc then snapped the reins again. "Just where are these belongings of yours?"

"A little ways across the river. It's not too far." She nibbled her lip and clenched her hands so tightly together in her lap that her knuckles turned white.

They rode back through town, receiving stares again, as they headed toward the river. Quinn shook his head. He hadn't been the center of so much attention since he and Anna had been jailed.

"Thank you for what you did—marrying me, I mean. I want you to know that I truly am innocent. This has all been a horrible mistake."

Quinn stared again at his wife, unable to believe how pretty she looked once she'd cleaned up. She seemed as if she was struggling not to squirm. His heart jolted. She had blue eyes. In the dimness of the jail, he'd thought they were gray or even brown. He'd always hoped if he married that he'd wed a woman with eyes the color of the summer sky. A tiny flame deep within him sparked to life.

Her long black hair was pinned up in a womanly fashion, but he'd seen it down, hanging clear to her waist, and that's the picture that remained in his mind. Her skin wasn't porcelain white like one of Anna's dolls but had been kissed by the sun into a light brown. He wouldn't admit it out loud, but he'd done all right for himself.

Still, she couldn't be anywhere near his age. "Just how old are you, ma'am?"

"Nineteen."

He scowled. There was nearly a decade difference in their ages. "You're mighty young."

"What about you?"

"Twenty-eight."

She raised a hand to her chest. "My, but you're positively ancient."

Her teasing made him grin; then he sobered. "That a problem for you?"

"No. Is it a problem for you?"

He pursed his lips. She was young enough to take care of him in his old age. He nearly chuckled out loud. "I reckon not."

In her efforts to stay away from him, she'd scooted clear over to the right of the seat. She'd seemed apprehensive of the men in town who'd watched her outside the general store. Did he frighten her? "You can relax. I won't hurt you."

Her gaze darted to his, and he could read the questions in her eyes. Eyes that he could get used to staring into. He focused on the trail ahead. They passed the old meat processing plant that the Marquis de Mores had closed nearly a decade earlier. The giant building with its sky-high smokestack was a sad reminder of a failed dream.

"What is that place? It looks empty."

"It is. A French marquis came here back in '83 when the big cattle bonanza was still in full swing. He had a vision to butcher cattle here and ship refrigerated beef back East." He looked over his left shoulder. "Don't know if you can still see it, but that big two-story building up there in the hills was his home."

Sarah glanced in the direction he pointed. "So, what happened?"

Quinn shrugged. "Two bad winters all but destroyed the herds of cattle around here. And with the competition from other beef producers, the marquis went bust and took his family back to New York, or wherever it was they came from."

"That's sad." Sarah looked back at the abandoned plant.

That was life, as far as he was concerned. Some benefited from living in the Badlands but most were victims of the harsh winters and hot summers in one way or another. Still, he was grateful for the town the marquis started. Without Medora, it would be a long trip to the next closest town.

They crossed the river and rode on in companionable silence for the next few miles. He had to admit he kind of liked having a pretty woman at his side, and he couldn't wait to see his grandma's expression when he returned with a blue-eyed brunette instead of a redhead. But what was he going to tell her? How could he explain that he married a stranger just to get her out of jail? It sounded ridiculous when he thought of it that way.

He just couldn't leave that red-faced waif in that dark cell.

Maybe he'd been quick to marry, but he didn't have time to socialize and court a woman like they wanted to be. He didn't even know a woman he would have fancied courting. But now he had a wife.

It sounded weird even in his mind. His wife. Sarah McFarland.

"Over there's where I found the horse I rode into town. It was just standing off the road, eating grass. I was tired and nobody answered my call when I hollered. I figured it must have gotten loose in town and wandered out here."

He looked where she pointed, and sure enough, the grass was broken down as if a large animal had walked through it. He started to turn his head back to the road when he spotted a pile of manure. So a horse *had* been there. Sarah's story was far-fetched, but maybe she was telling the truth. But even if she'd found the horse, it still didn't account for the gold she had in her possession.

She worried her lower lip and fidgeted in the seat for the next fifteen minutes, always scanning the area on his side of the wagon. Was she looking for something?

A short while later, she motioned to his left. "Pull over there, and I'll get my, uh. . .belongings."

Quinn glanced around, wondering where she could have stored them. There was nothing but rocky buttes, ridges, and grass for as far as he could see. He stopped the wagon and set the brake, but his wife scurried down without waiting for his help. Picking up his rifle, he stood, watching her shuffle down the incline beside the road. He jumped to the ground, not liking how she trotted off unarmed into the wilds without any hesitation. Didn't she know any number of critters might be down there, awaiting prey for dinner? Was she trying to ditch him and get away?

He was halfway to her when she disappeared into a rickety old shack he just noticed. He heard high-pitched squeals and quickened his steps. Voices? Someone else was in the shanty. Quinn slowed down and raised his rifle. Could she be leading him into a trap? Had she led him straight to her outlaw den? If so, they sure weren't very successful outlaws.

His wife's soft voice carried out the door. He couldn't hear her words, but the happy tone didn't indicate she was plotting his demise. Still, he took cover behind a pine and kept his Winchester ready.

She stepped outside carrying a rusty rifle pointed toward the ground and a faded old quilt in one arm. Her belongings, he surmised. That's what she'd made all that fuss over?

Behind her, a young boy and even younger girl stepped out of the shanty. Their gazes darted from side to side. Quinn's concern about outlaws shifted to cold shock. His mouth sagged open, and he couldn't do a thing about it. There was no chance on earth that those were her children. Although both kids had the same blue eyes as Sarah's, the boy's hair was brown while the little girl's was blond. Quinn's mouth went dry. These were her *belongings*? His wife had deceived him. He scowled. "What's going on?"

"Children, this is my husband, Quinn McFarland."

Both of the kids gawked at him. He steeled himself not to squirm under their scrutiny.

"This is Ryan, and this is Elizabeth." Sarah touched each child's head in a loving caress. "Ryan is eight, and Beth is six. They're my brother and sister."

His anger burned like a grassfire in a heavy wind. Hadn't Will mentioned something about some children? So she hadn't been lying about them either. No wonder she was so desperate to get out of jail that she'd agreed to marry him. He was a fool to hope maybe she'd seen something in him that she'd liked. That he was a cavalier knight who'd swooped in and rescued the innocent maiden. Instead, she'd played him like a pawn on a chess board.

"Are we going to live with him?" The little girl's worried gaze darted between Quinn and Sarah.

Sarah nodded her head and smiled softly at the child. "Yes—"

"No!" Quinn hollered.

The color drained from Sarah's face as she stared at him with disbelief.

The little girl started crying and grabbed Sarah's skirt. "Don't leave us again. You promised you'd never leave me, but you did."

The boy crossed his skinny arms and glared at him. Quinn felt like an egg-sucking dog. Like a low-down, yellow-bellied snake. What kind of a man refuses to care for needy children? Especially a man who'd helped raise his own siblings. They'd just caught him off guard, was all. He'd barely gotten his twin sister and brother raised and married off. He hadn't wanted a wife, and now he was strapped with two more children. And he didn't like losing control of his life. His throat closed as if he was the one with a hangman's noose tightening around it.

"No?" Sarah's eyes sparked like blue fire. Beth whimpered and sniffled into her sister's skirt. "How can you refuse to care for two orphans?"

Hadn't he just asked himself the same question? He ducked his head, shamed by his outburst, his shoulders weighted with guilt. "Sorry. Of course they can come. I was just taken off guard. Is that all of your stuff—or do you have any more surprises for me?"

Sarah furrowed her brow. "That's everything."

He stepped forward and took her bundle and rusty rifle before she decided to turn the weapon on him.

"You two get in the back of the wagon." Sarah motioned the children up the hill.

"I want to sit with you." The girl's whine sent a chill down Quinn's spine. What had he gotten himself into?

But what else could he do? It was a miracle the two younguns were still alive after a stormy night alone in that old shack. Why, the door didn't even look as if it closed.

The boy—Brian? Rowan? What was his name?—scowled at Quinn as he stomped past him.

Quinn pursed his lips. He deserved the boy's ire. He'd probably spent the last day and night protecting and comforting his younger sister while worrying himself half sick about his older one. The scrawny lad looked exhausted and dark rings shadowed his eyes. When was the last time they'd all had a good meal? Or a bath?

He swung the wagon back toward Medora with Sarah and her two siblings aboard. How could a man lose control of his life so fast? Quinn hunched over, resting his elbows on his knees. He peeked in the back of the buckboard. The girl had curled up on the worn quilt, but the boy sat with his back against the side of the wagon, his arms on his knees, glaring at Quinn.

Well, he certainly deserved the boy's contempt after his foolish outburst. But any man would be angry to marry a woman and find out she had two kids she hadn't told him about. It didn't matter that they were siblings and not her own children. They were a responsibility he hadn't bargained on. He needed more children on the ranch about as much as he needed a three-legged horse.

But wouldn't his grandmother be delighted to have children in the house again? He just wasn't sure how she'd respond to him marrying a woman in jail. She'd probably say he deserved the kids after marrying in such haste. This was all the fault of Miss Zerelda von Something-or-other. If she hadn't agreed to come in the first place, or if she'd at least honored her agreement and married him, none of this would have happened. Maybe it was all a bad dream and he'd wake up in the morning with everything back to normal.

He sniffed a laugh. Yeah, sure. And tomorrow the sky would be green.

❧

Sarah was as angry as a hen drenched in dishwater. How dare Quinn say her siblings couldn't come with them? Yes, he'd changed his mind rather quickly and looked plenty chagrined for his angry eruption, but it was obvious to her that he didn't want the children. Well, like it or not, he was stuck with them. She could only hope he wouldn't make them all miserable.

An hour later, out of the corner of her eye, Sarah saw Beth moving. Her sister had been asleep since shortly after leaving the shack. Beth jerked up, and her frantic gaze darted around until it settled on Sarah. She smiled, hoping to soothe her little sister's concern.

"I gots to go, Sissy."

Quinn glanced sideways and sighed. "Whoa, hold up." The wagon stopped, and he set the brake. He lifted his hat and swiped the sweat off his brow with his sleeve. "Do your business quickly. We need to be getting home."

He climbed down, strode to the back of the wagon, and reached out for Beth. She spun around, shinnied over Ryan and the crates of supplies, and flew into Sarah's lap. If Sarah hadn't still been so angry, she might have laughed at her husband's surprised expression. She set her sister aside, climbed out of the wagon without waiting for his help, and then lifted Beth down. Ryan stood and stretched then jumped over the side of the wagon and walked out into the tall grass.

"Watch out for prairie rattlers."

Sarah's heart pounded, and she glanced around. She might tolerate mice but snakes were another thing. Ryan jogged a ways past them, and Sarah and Beth finished quickly.

"He don't like us, does he?" Beth looked up at Sarah as

they walked back to the wagon, and she realized her sister wasn't limping.

She turned and knelt down. "It's not that, sweetie. I didn't tell him about you, and he was just surprised. Men sometimes get angry if you surprise them."

"Like Uncle Harlan did?"

Sarah nodded. A shiver ran down her back as she remembered her uncle's short temper. She rubbed her right wrist—the one he liked to grab hold of when he wanted to scold her for some minor thing she or the children had done.

"Papa never got angry."

Sarah smiled, glad her sister only had good memories of their father. He had never hurt them, but he'd shouted a time or two when she and Ryan had done something stupid. "Just give Mr. McFarland time, and he'll see how sweet you are. Then he won't be able to keep from loving you like I do."

Sarah hugged Beth, hoping desperately that what she'd said was true. Would Quinn's grandmother be happy with her and the children? Or would she be angry at the big surprise her grandson would soon be popping on her?

"How's your ankle?"

Beth stared at the ground. "It don't hurt no more."

Sarah twisted her lips. Beth probably faked her twisted ankle just so she didn't have to walk so far. Her sister might be small but she was clever. "Why don't you pick some wildflowers while we wait for Ryan?" Beth nodded and skipped toward a nearby patch of flowers. Sarah glanced over her shoulder. Where was that boy? "Ryan?"

"Coming." He plowed through the grass like a crazed bull and stopped in front of her. "Why were you gone all night? Beth was scared during that storm."

"It's a long story." Sarah sighed. "Just know that I had no choice about returning before now. I'll tell you later, but we'd better not keep Mr. McFarland waiting. He's anxious to get home."

"I watched over Beth. Even held her last night when she was scared of the dark and crying for you."

Sarah smiled and tugged her brother into her arms. "I appreciate that. I knew I could depend on you. I'm sorry I scared you and didn't get back before dark. Just wait until you hear what happened."

"Tell me now."

She turned Ryan back toward the wagon, determined not to rile her husband any more this day. Every man had his limit, and she sure didn't want to find out what Quinn's was. Beth scurried around gathering yellow, scarlet, and purple flowers. When she'd gathered a handful, she hurried over to Quinn. He checked one of the horses' hooves and stood, patting the large animal's rump.

Beth nibbled her lip and watched him. When he turned her way, she lifted the flowers up to him. "These are for you."

His questioning gaze sought out Sarah's, and she held her breath. Quinn stooped down and rested his forearms on his knees. "Why, thank you, ma'am. Nobody ever gave me flowers before."

Beth turned and flashed Sarah a wide smile. Quinn lifted her sister into the buckboard without complaint. Ryan climbed in back and glared at Quinn again.

He sniffed the flowers. "Well," he said, as Sarah approached, "looks like I've won over one of them at least."

six

The buckboard jostled and dipped to the left into the dried rut of a previous wagon, then bounced free of it a few feet down the trail. Sarah's shoulder bumped Quinn's, and he peered sideways at her. He ought to be furious with her deception, but now that he'd gotten over his surprise, the honest truth was he admired her for caring so much for her siblings that she'd marry a stranger. Still, his pride took another shot that she hadn't wanted to marry him because she liked what she saw.

He glanced in the back of the wagon. Ryan and Beth were both asleep. "I've got a young brother and sister, too."

His wife's blue gaze darted in his direction. Her dark brows lifted.

"Twins, actually. Adam and Anna will be twenty-five in another month. Both are married."

"Didn't you mention that one has a baby?"

"Adam, and his wife is Mariah." A smile tugged at Quinn's lip as he thought of Jonathon. "They live at the ranch when they aren't traveling."

"Traveling?" Sarah picked up the canteen lying on the floorboard and took a swig.

"Adam is a gifted artist. They tour the West, and he draws pictures for a man in Chicago who owns a gallery. Mariah writes dime novels."

His wife choked and nearly spewed the water she'd been drinking. "You're teasing. She does not."

"Honest. She does." He lifted a hand in the air and couldn't help grinning at Sarah's expression.

"I've never heard of such a thing. It sounds so exciting."

Quinn shrugged. "I've read a few of her novels. They're not bad, even though she generally has a woman saving the day."

Sarah dabbed at her mouth and scowled. "What's wrong with that?"

"Not too realistic if you ask me."

She didn't say anything but looked out over the Badlands. He'd like to know what she was thinking—if she was one of those women who thought they could outdo a man. Hadn't he just saved her? And in doing so rescued her siblings from certain death?

"What about your sister? Does she live on the ranch, too?"

"No, she and her husband live on his ranch down south, 'bout a day's ride from here." Quinn guided the horses off the main trail and onto the one leading to the ranch. Yesterday's storms were long gone, and the sun now shone down in full force. He lifted his hat, swiped the sweat from his brow, and scowled when he realized Sarah wasn't wearing a hat. He'd have to see if one of Anna's old ones was still around or buy her a new hat next time he came to town.

What was he going to tell his grandma about her?

"Does your sister have any children?"

He shook his head. "Brett and Anna just married last fall, and several months after that, Adam and Mariah's cute little son was born on the ranch."

"How old is he?"

"A couple of months. He was born in March."

"I imagine you must enjoy him."

Quinn nodded. "Yeah, but I haven't seen them since early last month." He peeked at his wife and thought again how pretty she had cleaned up. He'd looked right past her in the store, not once thinking the pretty lady at the counter could be her. Yes sir, he'd done all right for himself.

But what about her? Women had funny notions when it

came to weddings and marrying. Had she been disappointed in her only choice of husband? If Will had given her a choice of men, would she have picked him or someone else?

"Would you tell me about your grandmother?"

"Sure," he said, surprised that she'd asked. He leaned forward, elbows on his knees, and held the reins loosely in his hands. "My grandma and grandpa moved from Texas to Bismarck about a year after my dad moved us up here. Grandpa died four years ago, but Grandma stayed in Bismarck because of her friends and church. About a year and a half ago, she fell and broke her leg real bad. My mom left the ranch and went to live with Grandma so she could care for her. Mom never came home much after that."

"Must have been hard. I sure miss my mother."

Pursing his lips, Quinn watched a hawk circling in the sky. After his father's death, he and his ma had gotten closer because they had to work together to keep the ranch running. He had missed her when she left them to tend Grandma, and now she was gone forever. "Ma died several months ago."

Sarah gasped and turned toward him in the seat. "I'm so sorry. What happened? I mean. . .you don't have to talk about it unless you want to."

Quinn stared straight ahead, ignoring the compassion in her eyes. He'd cried at the funeral and didn't want to go down that road again—especially not in front of his new wife. "She took sick with a fever. It was so fast it stunned us all. I brought Grandma to the ranch to live with me after that. She didn't really want to come, but I didn't want her all alone and didn't have time to be traveling back and forth to Bismarck." He didn't mention that he hadn't wanted to be alone either.

"I'm sorry for your loss." Sarah peeked over her shoulder at the children in back. "We lost our parents when the farmhouse burned down in late April. The children were at school, and I'd gone into town on an errand. We don't know what happened." She turned away and dabbed at her eyes.

Quinn thought about the irony of the situation. He was struggling with his own mother's death when about the same time the woman who would become his wife was enduring a similar loss, only worse.

Sarah's shoulders quivered. He leaned forward and looked at her. She turned farther away, dabbed her face, then hiked up her chin. He considered putting his arm around her, but she'd already gotten control of her emotions. Good. That strength of backbone would do her well out here.

"Sorry about your folks." Quinn steered the buckboard onto the trail leading to the Rocking M and pulled the wagon to a halt. He waved a hand in the air. "As far as you can see in three directions is Rocking M land."

"You're blessed, Mr. McFarland. The bank took our farm after the fire."

He wondered how they'd gotten by but figured that was a topic for another day. "Call me Quinn. Mr. McFarland was my pa."

Her cheeks turned a rosy red. "And you must call me Sarah."

He liked her name. It was a strong name. Sarah, as in the wife of Abraham, mother of the Hebrew nation. He clicked the horses forward. Abraham and Sarah had been united until death, but could a marriage such as his last? Maybe he'd be better off not getting his hopes up. Sarah obviously married him for one reason only—to get out of jail so she could get back to her siblings. He'd been a loner pretty much ever since his pa had died. It was best he cut his losses and protect his heart.

"Grandma hasn't been well since Ma's death. It took something out of her to watch her only child die. Having you and the children there will be an encouragement. I want you to know that I don't expect anything from you—

except to care for Grandma. We'll think of this as a business arrangement." He glanced at Sarah, but she stared straight ahead, her lips pressed together. "I don't want you to think you're stuck with me forever. Once Grandma passes, I'll give you enough money so that you and the children can start over somewhere else."

&

Shock rolled through Sarah, forcing her to look away from her husband for fear she might cry. Had he found her so lacking already, without even giving her a fair try, that he was ready to be rid of her the first chance he got? Or was it because she hadn't been honest about the children?

She crushed a fold in her skirt as disappointment surged through her. *Why, God? You freed me from jail and provided a home for us. So why does he wish to be rid of me so fast?*

She blinked, pushing the tears away. This was just another obstacle she'd have to climb over. In the meantime, the children would have a home and food to eat. And hopefully, Uncle Harlan wouldn't find them. At least her husband—she nearly choked at the word—would provide for them to start over.

If only they could find a permanent home. She was tired of not knowing what was ahead. She longed for security and thought she'd found it with Quinn. But it wasn't to be.

"Tell me about your family." Quinn glanced at her then focused on the trail ahead.

Her heart ached so badly that she didn't want to talk to him. Some protector he turned out to be. Still, if she remained silent, he'd suspect something was wrong and most likely question her about that. She'd rather talk about her parents.

She peeked over her shoulder at the children still asleep in the back then faced forward again. "My father had a farm outside of Grand Forks. He grew mainly sugar beets."

"Got downwind of a sugar beet farm once. Phew. That's stinky stuff." He waved his hand in front of his nose.

"I can't say that I miss that much." But she did miss her parents. How could life change so quickly? One day she was an innocent young woman looking to capture the eye of tall, blond Peder Ericksen. The next day she was homeless with two grieving children to provide for. The neighbors who took them in had been kind and sympathetic, but when those same neighbors sought to separate them, Sarah asked Peder to marry her. She'd never forget the shock in his pale eyes. When he said no, they'd caught the first train heading west in hopes the kind uncle she remembered from her youth would give them sanctuary.

She pressed her lips together. How could a man change so much in a few years?

Should she tell Quinn they might be in danger? That her outlaw uncle could very well come hunting for them?

Show me what to do, Lord.

"I don't guess you're used to all these hills after living in the flatlands."

"No, but I like it here. The landscape is so interesting, and the view over every hill is a little different." She looked out across the rugged terrain. Flat-topped buttes stood guardian over valleys of rocky grasslands. Covering her brows to block the sun, she stared at some black dots moving in the distance, a cloud of dust following. Buffalo. She'd never seen one before but heard they weren't nearly as abundant as they used to be.

Quinn nudged her arm. "Look over there on that far hill."

She turned and scanned where he pointed. "What are they? Deer?"

"Elk."

"At first glance, this place looks barren, but there are many surprises." Wildflowers danced in the light breeze, a pleasant contrast to the browns of the rocky hills. She heard a rustling behind her, and Beth crawled up to the back of the seat and leaned her arms on it.

"Are we about there? I'm hungry."

"It's not much farther. We have a cook name Elke. She can fix a snack to hold you until suppertime."

"Elke's a funny name."

Sarah spun around on the seat. "Beth, we don't poke fun at people's names. That was rude."

Beth hung her head for a moment then grinned. "Well, it is funny."

Quinn chuckled, and Sarah glared at him. He didn't need to be encouraging Beth.

"Elke is German. She's the cousin of our previous cook, who went to live with my sister when she moved to her new husband's ranch."

"What is Elke's last name?" Beth asked.

Quinn scratched his head and honestly looked perplexed. "You know, I'm not sure. I've just called her Elke ever since she arrived."

"Well, we will find out, and you will call her by her last name. Is that clear, Beth?"

Her sister nibbled her lower lip and nodded. Quinn looked as if he'd like to argue with Sarah but wisely kept his mouth shut.

"What's that up there?" Beth stuck her arm between Sarah and Quinn and pointed.

"That's the sign to the Rocking M Ranch. We've been on my land for a while, but that's the official entrance."

"It looks funny standing there all by itself. Where's the fence?"

Sarah's eyes widened. If Beth kept this up they would never make it to the ranch house.

"I suppose it does look odd," Quinn said. "But most of

the land out here isn't fenced. My ma wanted a sign, so my brother and I put one up."

They drove under the sign that was supported by two tall beams. Sarah enjoyed the quiet of nature after being in the noisy town. Even better were the wide-open spaces and the feel of the sun on her face. A cool breeze kept her from getting too hot, but she wished she'd thought to buy a bonnet at the general store. Maybe she could make one for her and Beth if there was enough fabric left after making Beth a dress.

They crested another hill, and she sucked in a breath at the sight of the huge cabin that came into view.

"Is that your house?" Beth stood and leaned forward over the back of the bench. "It's really big."

Quinn nodded and a satisfied look encompassed his handsome face. "Yep, that's home."

"I've never seen a cabin so large," Beth whispered as if in awe.

Sarah experienced the same amazement at her first view of the cozy home situated in a valley that was surrounded on all sides by tall buttes. This was a place that cried home—shelter. The safe haven she longed for, but it was only temporary. Why would God send them to this place only to have it taken away once they'd become settled?

"Pa wanted Ma to have a home she could be proud of. We had a big house back in Texas, and he wanted her to have a large one here. It wasn't easy, though; we had to have much of the wood shipped in since there are so few trees around here. It took a lot of hauling."

Her father had provided a nice home for their mother and them, but it was all gone in a puff of smoke. She never knew how fast things could change.

Now that they were actually here, nervousness twittered in Sarah's stomach. She crushed the fold of her skirt in her hand. How long would they be here? A few weeks? Months?

Would Quinn's grandmother send her packing when she learned that Sarah had been in jail?

Sarah lifted her chin and took a deep breath. One thing for certain, she was going to do everything possible to see that Quinn's grandmother recovered from whatever it was that ailed her and that she lived a long, healthy life. Then maybe they could stay long enough for Quinn to come to care for them. And if he cared, maybe then he'd keep them.

seven

With home in sight, the team picked up their pace and headed for the barn. Quinn still didn't know how to explain to his grandma everything that had happened. He didn't want to upset her and cause her to be afraid when she learned Sarah had been in jail.

Then again, Sarah was hardly intimidating. No, her wide, expressive eyes took in everything and emanated an innocence that couldn't be faked. Still. . .how could he explain why he married a woman who'd been jailed for bank robbery? He hardly knew why himself.

Maybe it was the fear in her eyes. How they pleaded for someone to believe she was innocent. Or maybe it was that long dark hair swirling past her shoulders down to her waist. The only woman he'd seen with her hair down had been his sister, and that was hardly the same thing.

Something in him had wanted to be her hero. To rescue her.

He'd been a fool. A man alone for too long. He'd given in to a moment of insanity. How could any good come from such a harebrained idea?

He guided the wagon toward the barn. "Whoa. . ." He set the brake and turned on the seat to face Sarah before one of the ranch hands showed up. Ryan sat up and rubbed his eyes and looked around; his anger was subdued for the moment, replaced by open curiosity.

Beth jumped up and down. "Sissy. . .I got. . ."

Sarah looked at him. "Where is your necessary?"

"She can use the one behind the house." He nudged his chin toward the cabin.

Sarah looked at Ryan, and the boy rolled his eyes. "Oh, all right. C'mon, Beth." He helped his sister off the wagon and the two walked toward the house. Beth glanced over her shoulder as if checking to make sure Sarah wasn't leaving.

"This is going to sound crazy, but I reckon you need to know this." Quinn lifted his hat and ran his fingers through his hair. "Yesterday morning, my grandma informed me that I was to ride into town and meet my mail-order bride at the train station. That was the first I'd heard about her."

Sarah's eyes widened, and she opened her mouth but didn't say anything. What was she thinking?

He plunged ahead before he lost his nerve. "She didn't show up. But there was a letter at the post office saying she'd changed her mind." Quinn looked away so she wouldn't see his embarrassment. Where were the ranch hands? He yanked off his hat and fiddled with the brim, working up his nerve to continue.

Sarah laid her hand on his arm, drawing his attention back to her. "I'm sorry. That must have made you feel terrible."

He didn't want her compassion. He was a crusty ol' rancher. Too hardened by life to need a woman. And yet something within him longed for Sarah to like him—to need him.

He looked down, hating that the sting of the bride's rejection still pained him. "I want you to pretend to be the mail-order bride."

Sarah's brows lifted in surprise but quickly dipped down into a scowl. Quinn held up his hand. "Hear me out before you say no. Grandma hasn't been well since Ma died. I'm afraid if I tell her you were in jail that it would cause her undue worry and make her worse."

His wife's pretty lips pressed together so tightly that they turned white. She breathed loud breaths through her nose like a riled up mustang. Finally, she looked at him. "I'm afraid I can't pretend to be your mail-order bride. It would be lying."

Irritation surged through him. "Seems a little late to be getting self-righteous." Hadn't she deceived him just this morning?

"I'm not self-righteous. I don't believe in telling falsehoods." She stuck that cute little nose in the air.

"Uh-huh. And I suppose you always refer to your brother and sister as your 'belongings'?"

A rosy pink stained her cheeks and she looked away. "I told that sheriff I had siblings, but he didn't believe me. He thought it was just a ploy to get out of jail."

"But you didn't tell me. You should have said something before we married. It's a lot to expect a man to take on two children. He has a right to know about that before he marries." His gut twisted. Sheriff Jones had mentioned something about two siblings.

She spun toward him. "And would you have married me if you'd known?"

Quinn resisted the urge to back away from the fire in her gaze. "Maybe." He shrugged. "We'll never know now, will we?"

Sarah looked down, suddenly contrite. "I'm sorry. But I couldn't take a chance that you might change your mind. I had to get out of that jail and back to Ryan and Beth. Their lives were at stake. Can't you understand that?"

Yes, he could. Far more than she'd ever know. He'd been the only father figure for Adam and Anna since the accident that claimed their pa's life. He'd have done about anything to protect them from harm.

One of the horses whinnied as if questioning why he hadn't freed him of the harness. Quinn stood and shoved his hat back on. "I understand, Sarah. But surely you can see how I want to protect my grandmother from worrying about being safe in her own home—just because I married an outlaw."

"I am not an outlaw." Sarah stood, coming only up to the bottom of his nose. "And I do understand, but I still won't lie to your grandmother. That's no way to start a relationship."

Quinn heaved a sigh, thinking their own relationship had started with falsehoods, but kept that thought to himself. "All right. Let's go up to the house so you can meet her."

He jumped down and came around to help his wife. She placed her arms on his shoulders as he lifted her down. She didn't weigh much more than a newborn calf.

He started to let go but she held on, drawing his gaze to hers. "I won't tell her how we met. I will leave that up to you, if possible."

"Fair enough." Quinn offered her his arm and guided her toward the house. His esteem for her grew. He'd asked a stupid, impulsive thing of her. He didn't believe in telling falsehoods either and had surprised himself by asking her to do so. The fact that she'd refused elevated his opinion of her. Maybe she'd been telling the truth all along?

❧

Disappointment weighted down Sarah's shoulders as anxiety swirled in her stomach. How could Quinn have asked her to lie to his grandmother? She'd thought him to be a man of fine character. He hadn't leered at her like many of the other men in town had—at least once they'd decided not to lynch her. And he married her when he didn't have to.

Why should it bother her so much? Most people lied every day. But that wasn't how she'd been raised, and in her heart, she knew telling falsehoods was wrong.

She turned her thoughts to Quinn's grandmother. Would the woman be shocked to learn Sarah wasn't the mail-order bride she was expecting?

Beth ran around the side of the house, her gaze searching until it landed on Sarah. The girl hurried to her side. A door banged, and Ryan jogged toward them, apprehension in the boy's blue eyes. He looked longingly toward the barn. Ryan had always wanted a saddle horse, but his pa had said they could only afford the mule needed for pulling their plow. Maybe Quinn would teach him how to ride.

"Listen," she stooped and whispered, "don't mention Uncle Harlan or his gold for now."

The children both nodded, and their footsteps echoed on the wooden porch. Quinn opened the door and stepped aside to allow her to pass through first. Sarah smiled at him, knowing many men would have plowed inside without being gentlemanly.

The pungent scent of something cooking hung in the air, reminding her of how little she'd eaten in the past few days. Her eyes took a moment to adjust to the dimness of the room. Beth took her hand and leaned against Sarah's skirt. A nice-sized parlor held western-style furniture that Sarah assumed must have accompanied the family from Texas. The horsehair sofa looked old but still serviceable. A low, rectangular table sat in front of the sofa, with two chairs on the other side of the table. The parlor connected with the dining room, making one very large room. A table with seating for ten people boasted a vase holding colorful wildflowers. Too bad the flowers Beth gave Quinn had already wilted.

The door shut behind her, and Quinn strode past them. Ryan came around to Sarah's other side and stood close but didn't hang on her like Beth did.

"Grandma? I'm home."

Home. If only this comfortable cabin could become their home, too.

"Coming." A gray-haired woman glided into the room, a big smile on her face. Her gaze landed on Sarah, and her smile faltered.

She doesn't like me. Sarah wanted to flee out the door, but there was no place to run to. They were stuck here, no matter how bad things might be. Quinn's grandma looked at him and raised her white brows.

He shuffled his feet but held her gaze. "Grandma, this is Sarah. My wife."

Surprise widened the woman's eyes then the charming smile returned. "Welcome, dear. You don't know how happy I am to meet you." She hurried forward, not looking sick at all, and held out her hand.

Sarah took it, and the older woman laid her other hand atop Sarah's. "I've prayed long and hard for you, my dear."

Sarah glanced up at Quinn. He actually looked as if he was blushing, but she couldn't tell for certain. She turned back to his grandma. "I'm Sarah Oak—"

Quinn cleared his throat, and Sarah realized her mistake. She smiled. "I'm Sarah McFarland, ma'am. It's a pleasure to meet you." The new name sounded odd on her lips.

"I'm Martha Miles, but you may call me Martha—or Grandma—whichever you'd like. And who are these fine youngsters?"

Sarah patted Beth's head. "This is my sister, Beth, and my brother, Ryan."

Martha clapped her hands together. "I'm so delighted that there will be children in this house again. Where is your luggage?"

"I'll get their things if you can show them to their rooms." Quinn glanced at Sarah. "I need to tend to the horses then I'll bring in your *belongings*." A soft smile tugged at one corner of his lips.

Was he teasing her? Surely not.

"Come this way. We have enough bedrooms that you can each use one for now. Of course once Adam and Mariah return, things will be more crowded." She opened a door to a room that held a double bed. Several framed drawings of cattle scenes decorated the wall. There was one chair as well as a small desk.

"Ryan, this is Adam's room. You may sleep in here for now."

Her brother's eyes widened. "By myself?"

Sarah wasn't sure if he was frightened or in awe.

Grandma Miles nodded. "When Adam and Mariah return, you will need to share a room with your sister, or maybe you'd prefer to sleep in the bunkhouse with the ranch hands."

Her somber brother actually smiled.

Across the hall, they entered a small whitewashed room. A colorful quilt decorated the single bed and matching curtains hung on the lone window. A small wardrobe sat in one corner of the room and a wingback chair in the other. Sharing the small bed with Beth, who wriggled in her sleep, would be awkward, but they'd slept on far worse in the past few months. Maybe she could talk Ryan into switching rooms so she and Beth could have the larger bed, but she doubted he'd want this room, which looked as if it was decorated for a girl.

Grandma patted the bed and gazed at Beth. "This will be your room, sweetheart. It was my granddaughter Anna's before she married."

Beth's brow crinkled. "But I want to stay with Sarah."

Grandma leaned over. "Sarah will be just down the hall. She's married now and needs to sleep with her husband."

Sarah was certain her eyes must have widened as much as Beth's. Her heart throbbed. Why hadn't she considered that before? How was she going to get out of this quagmire?

Beth leaned against Sarah, and she realized she needed to comfort the girl. "This is our home now. I'm not leaving you again. I promise."

Beth looked as if she wanted to remind Sarah that she'd made that promise before but hadn't kept it.

"Can you imagine this whole room is yours? I've never even had a room of my own before." Sarah patted her sister's head.

Beth considered that and looked around. "Can I leave the lantern lit when I sleep?"

"Of course you can, dear."

"And the door open?"

Martha smiled. "If it makes you feel better, you certainly may. Would you like to try out the bed?"

Beth nodded and reached for the white metal frame. Sarah grabbed her sister's shoulder. "Perhaps it would be better to wait until she's had a bath."

Grandma Miles ran her gaze over the child and pressed her lips together. "You might be right. Let me show you to your room, then I'll have Elke—she's our cook and helps with other things we need—heat up some water for you to bathe in."

Sarah followed the older woman down a short hallway and through an open door. A large bed filled one wall of the room, and Sarah swallowed. She had to force herself not to gawk at it. Curtains fluttered at the open window, drawing her attention. She nearly gasped at the view. Coal black cattle grazed peacefully throughout the wide valley. One butte looked as if someone had sliced off the slide, revealing colorful layers of orange, tan, and even black. Shadows crept along the ground, eating up the light, where the sun had started to set behind the tall buttes.

She heard a rustling and turned back to survey the room. A sofa rested across from an unlit fireplace, and a large wardrobe all but covered one wall. A braided rug in blues, greens, and white warmed the wooden floor and gave the room a cozy touch.

Grandma Miles picked up a housecoat and some slippers. "The room belonged to Quinn's parents. He insisted I move in here when I first arrived, but I never liked this room. It's far too big, and I have trouble getting into that high bed."

Sarah wasn't sure where this conversation was leading so she remained silent.

"I'll move my things into Quinn's room. You two will be sharing this one now."

Quinn halted in the hall outside his grandmother's room. Sarah stood looking out the window. Why was she in there? He assumed she would stay in Anna's room or maybe Sarah and Beth could share the double bed in Adam and Mariah's room for now. He kicked open the door to his room. Sarah could stay there, and he'd move to the bunkhouse. He set the two large bundles his wife had purchased onto his bed. Now he understood why she'd bought so much fabric. She must have planned on making her siblings some clothes. What they wore wouldn't be good enough for piecings in one of his grandma's quilts.

He stopped in the hall, wondering what the two women were talking about. Beth clung to Sarah's skirt, but Ryan was nowhere to be seen. He hoped the boy wasn't getting into trouble. Quinn shook his head. He had some fences to mend where Ryan was concerned. The boy still hadn't forgiven him for his initial outburst.

"You and Quinn will be sharing this room now."

Quinn's heart jolted at his grandmother's words. Oh no! Why hadn't he considered that?

Of course his grandma would assume the newlyweds would room together. He ran his hand over the back of his neck. Sarah wouldn't like this development. And neither did he.

"I don't want you to have to move on my accord, Martha. I can sleep with Beth for the time being."

"Nonsense," Quinn said, stepping into his parents' bedroom. "A man and wife should share a room." He hoped he sounded sincere when he felt anything but that.

Sarah turned and stared at him. He swallowed hard. If he insisted they not share a room, Grandma would suspect things weren't on the up-and-up.

"I'll just move my things into your room." Grandma marched toward him, carrying her robe and slippers; a twinkle he hadn't seen since his mother's death danced in her brown eyes. "A redhead, huh?" she whispered as she passed. She deposited her things on his bed and turned. "While your wife and the children have their baths, I'll move your clothing into the big room."

Quinn nodded and started removing his clothes from the wardrobe. Grandma hurried out of the room and down the hall.

Sarah stopped just outside his door. "Do something. We can't share—" She looked down at Beth. "Sweetie, why don't you go see what Ryan is doing?" Beth glanced from Sarah to Quinn and back then walked toward her brother's room.

"We'll have to make the best of things, Sarah. I don't want Grandma thinking we're not a true married couple."

She leaned forward. "But we aren't. At least that's what you said. Have you changed your mind?"

Crossing her arms, his wife's eyes shot blue fire at him. Did she have any idea how pretty she was when she was angry? For a moment he almost changed his mind. He almost said he wanted a real marriage. But Sarah would leave one day—just like the siblings he'd raised. Just like the parents he'd loved so much. And he was the one who'd opened the door for her to go—once Grandma had passed. "We'll share this room, Sarah. We are married, after all."

eight

Sarah lifted her arms and allowed the new nightgown to fall over her body. She'd never had one so soft or so pretty. Oh, how good it felt to be clean again. But even better would be sleeping in a real bed after spending so many nights on a hard pallet. If not for the fact that Quinn expected to share that bed, things would be wonderful. But if not for her husband, they wouldn't even be at the Rocking M Ranch.

She spun around the big room. Never had she seen a bedroom this size. Why, it was even larger than the parlor had been at their farmhouse. Thoughts of her former home sobered her, and she dropped onto the sofa. A bear skin rug, complete with the head, lay between the fireplace and sofa. No fire burned, because the nights weren't cold enough. She stuck her feet underneath her gown, not wanting to touch the rug, and stared at the logs sitting ready for a match. *Lord, thank You for this wonderful home. Please heal Quinn's grandmother of what ails her so that we can stay here a long time. And help me. I don't know how to be a wife.*

A soft knock sounded at the door. Sarah jumped to her feet, raced across the room, leapt onto the bed, and crawled under the covers, her heart pounding.

"It's just me, dear. May I come in for a moment?" Grandma Miles pushed open the door and stuck her head in. "Oh, I didn't expect you'd be in bed already. We can talk tomorrow."

"No, please come in. I just—" It wouldn't do to explain that she was hiding from Quinn. "I was just thinking about today and all the changes it brought." She climbed off the bed and held out her hand. "Come and sit with me."

"I peeked at the children. Both are out cold." Martha smiled and ambled over to the sofa and sat down. She turned to face Sarah. "I wanted to let you know how happy I am that you're here."

"Thank you." Sarah held her quivering hands in her lap, hoping the older woman wouldn't ask how she'd met her grandson.

"Quinn is a good man. He's carried the burden for this family since his father died. He helped raise his siblings, and now he's caring for me." She looked down at her hands a moment; then a soft smile graced her wrinkled face. "I'm glad he has someone to take care of him now."

Not knowing what to say, Sarah remained quiet. Her gaze darted to the partially open door, and she picked a pillow off the sofa and held it against her chest. "I'll do my best to make Quinn happy and to help you."

Grandma patted her hand. "I'm sure you will. I'll admit that I'm curious how you and my grandson came to be married. It's obvious you aren't the mail-order bride I sent for, but that can wait for another day."

Sarah's heart skipped a beat. So she knew without being told that Sarah wasn't the bride she'd been expecting. What else did she know?

Grandma leaned in closer. "I do have to admit that I'm delighted to have the children here. They are such sweet things." She patted Sarah's hand. "Well, I'll let you get your rest. Tomorrow, I'll get my other things out of here. Then the room will be all yours and Quinn's. And I believe we might have some old clothes in a trunk somewhere that may fit your brother and sister."

She pushed up and walked to the door. "I'm so glad you're here, Sarah. I look forward to getting to know you better."

The door closed, and Sarah's heart warmed. She felt as if she'd made a new friend. And even better, Quinn's grandma didn't seem ill at all. Could there be something wrong that wasn't obvious? At least she could uphold the woman in her prayers and relieve her of some of the burden of the household chores.

Sarah moved to the door and peeked out. So far she'd seen no sign of her husband since supper. He'd shoved away from the table after the meal, muttering something about being behind on his chores. She'd wanted Ryan to help him, but the boy wouldn't leave her side.

A soft light shone out from under the door of Quinn's old room. Sarah tiptoed to Beth's room and peeked inside. The lantern had been turned down to a gentle glow, casting dancing shadows around the room. Beth lay on her side with her hands under her cheek. Sarah leaned over and kissed her then pulled up the colorful quilt.

She hurried to Ryan's room at the beginning of the hall. Stopping at his door, she peered into the dark parlor. Elke had fixed a delicious dinner of bratwurst, sauerkraut, applesauce, and braided bread with flavorful seeds in it. The scent still clung to the air. Sarah hoped she hadn't made a pig of herself by taking a second helping.

She opened Ryan's door and peeked in. The faint light of a half-moon illuminated his face as his soft snores filled the room. Sarah smiled and closed the door. When was the last time the children had rested so soundly—so worry free?

The front door opened, startling Sarah. She rushed down the hall, into her room, and dove under the covers. If she pretended to be asleep, maybe her husband wouldn't bother her tonight.

The thud of Quinn's boots moved closer, each step sending her pulse racing faster. She might be married, but she sure didn't feel married. His steps stopped at the door as if he was afraid to enter. Or maybe he was disappointed to find her sleeping. She carefully opened one eye a slit and peered at him.

He looked to be studying the floor. She hadn't gotten the impression he was a man of indecision, but he seemed hesitant to enter. Finally, he glanced over his shoulder toward his old bedroom and sighed. He stepped across the threshold and shut the door.

His footsteps softened as he crossed the braided rug at the end of the bed then clicked against the wooden floor next to where she lay under the covers. Her heart stampeded like a runaway horse. Could he hear it? Could he tell she was faking sleep?

With both eyes shut, she felt him watching her. Thank goodness she'd pulled the sheet up to her neck. The longer he stood there, the more she trembled. Finally, he walked toward the sofa, leaving behind the scent of leather and dust.

The sofa creaked as he lowered his heavy body onto it, and a boot flopped onto the floor, followed by another. She turned over and peeked out again. Quinn ran his hands through his thick hair, leaving swirls where the edges curled up. She wondered why he didn't keep his hair cut shorter like most curly-haired men would, but she liked it longer. Would it be as soft to the touch as her own was?

He stretched and then stood. She closed her eyes, lest he see her watching him, and heard him pad toward the chest of drawers. A soft *whoosh* sounded, the light faded, and darkness enveloped the room. Sarah's heart nearly jumped out of her chest. Would her husband come to bed now? She was as far on her side as she could be without falling off the edge, but her husband was a big man.

She heard a rustling near the fireplace and waited. Her ragged breathing would give her away if he was paying attention. He exhaled another sigh, and the room grew quiet.

Sarah waited, but he didn't come. He couldn't be sleeping on the sofa or it would be creaking under his weight. Then he must be lying on that smelly bear rug. Something in Sarah's stomach twisted at the unfairness of their situation. She was small. Her husband worked hard and needed his rest. Tomorrow, she'd sleep on the sofa—and hope and pray that his grandma didn't choose to pay her another before-bed visit.

⁂

Quinn rested his elbows on the table and sipped his coffee as he studied his makeshift family. Beth cast him shy smiles whenever he caught her eye. She was a darling. Her dark blond hair had been plaited and hung in two braids down the front of her faded dress. Had Sarah's dark hair been blond when she was a child?

Ryan still glared at him, but the hardness had left his blue eyes. The boy had no idea how much the two of them had in common. Having lost his own father, Quinn knew how Ryan was suffering. He wanted to make things easier for him. But how?

Silverware clinked against plates as the women and children finished eating their pancakes and sausage. Grandma dabbed at her lips and cleared her throat. "I think today we'll search that trunk in your bedroom, Sarah. I'm sure there are some clothes that we could alter to fit Ryan and Beth. That would give them something else to wear until we can make some new things out of the fabric that you got at the mercantile."

Beth's eyes lit up, but Ryan scowled and looked down at his shirt, as if he didn't see anything wrong with the patched flannel.

"Thank you. That would be nice. The children are in desperate need of new clothes." His wife's gaze darted in his direction then away, like a butterfly flitting from flower to flower.

She hadn't said anything about him sleeping on the floor, but then he'd been out of the room before sunup, so there'd been little chance for them to talk. He rolled his neck, working out the kinks. He was too young for his back to hurt, but after a night on the floor, he felt like an old-timer.

Halfway through the night, he'd seriously considered climbing out the window and finding a bed in the bunkhouse, but then the hands would wonder why he wasn't with his new bride. He didn't want to face the humiliation in those questions. Just their harmless teasing about being a newlywed was enough.

"What do you plan to do today, Quinn?"

He glanced at his grandma. Somehow the question didn't feel as innocent as it seemed. "Work. Same thing I always do."

"Perhaps there is something Ryan could do. He needs to learn the ways of a ranch if he's going to be living here."

Quinn caught the spark of hopefulness just before Ryan's eyes dulled again. The boy would be more trouble than he was worth, but Quinn's pa had taught <u>him</u>, and it was only fair that he teach Ryan. Quinn couldn't very well tell his grandma that the boy wouldn't be around all that long. "Sure. I can put him to work. That is, if it's all right with Sarah."

Ryan's head jerked toward his sister. There wasn't a doubt that he'd rather be helping Quinn than sorting and trying on old clothes. Maybe he'd do, after all.

"Of course, that would be fine. Ryan would love to learn to ride, and he knows some things. He did chores back at our farm." Sarah's eyes sparkled, nearly taking his breath away. He hadn't seen her so happy since she'd been reunited with the children.

"You'll have to do what I say. There are many things that can hurt someone who's not paying attention and doing what he's told. If you can't mind me, you'll have to stay in the house with the women."

Ryan's eyes narrowed. Quinn could tell the boy didn't like being ordered around, but he also didn't want to stay with the women all day. Finally, he nodded.

Quinn stood, hoping he wasn't making a mistake. His wife

would blame him if something happened to her brother. Ryan rose and followed him to the door. Quinn removed his hat from the peg on the wall and reached for the knob. Adam's old hat still hung on his peg. Quinn grabbed it and stuck it on Ryan's head. "My brother bought a new hat last time he was here. You can have his old one."

Ryan's eyes widened and a smile tugged at one corner of his mouth. He pushed the too-big hat up on his head.

Quinn looked at the boy's shoes. "We'll have to see if we can find you a pair of boots. All ranchers need boots."

The boy straightened and nodded. He glanced back over his shoulder at his sister with a half smile.

Sarah waved. "You work hard and be obedient."

Ryan nodded and looked up at Quinn. "What are we going to do?"

"Do you know how to ride?"

Ryan shook his head, but a sparkle danced in his eyes. "Not by myself. I rode our old mule back home, but Pa always led it or rode in front of me."

"Then let's start there."

❧

Two days later, Ryan ran into the kitchen. He skidded to a halt in front of Sarah. She looked up from where she was helping Beth make sugar cookies. "Sarah, I rode by myself today!"

Quinn followed Ryan, unable to keep the proud smile off his face at the boy's enthusiasm. Who would have thought teaching the boy to ride would be the thing to break down the walls between them?

Quinn crossed the room and snatched a cookie from the cooling rack. Instead of scolding him like Grandma or Elke would have, Sarah smiled, doing funny things to his insides.

"Thank you," she mouthed.

He nodded. He felt a tug on his pants and looked down. Beth stared up at him with big blue eyes. "I wanna ride a horse. It's not fair that Ryan gets to but I don't."

Quinn reached down, and Beth jumped up into his arms. The girl's unconditional love warmed his heart and made him wish her big sister felt the same. He took the end of her braid and tickled her cheek with it. Beth giggled and rubbed her face against his shirt.

"You won't like it. Horses are big and scary." Ryan scowled.

"Horses are big, but most of them aren't scary." Quinn lifted his brow at Ryan, hoping he'd understand that frightening his sister wasn't all right. He patted Beth's back. "If Sarah doesn't mind, I'll teach you to ride, too. My sister, Anna, is an excellent horsewoman."

"Truly?" Beth said, with awe in her voice. "Can I, Sissy?"

Sarah nodded. "It's probably a good idea for you to learn, but we'll have to do it at a time so as not to take the men away from their work."

"When's that?" Beth looked at Quinn.

"After dinner some evening."

Grandma entered the kitchen and picked up a platter of biscuits off the counter, her eyes twinkling. "Wash up, you two. Lunch is ready."

Quinn could tell she already loved her new family. She seemed to have twice the peppiness this week over last. Having Sarah and the kids here had been a huge boost to his grandma and seemed to have revived her spirits and her health. And she hadn't yet asked him how he came about marrying Sarah. But she would one day. He just hoped by then she'd be so in love with Sarah and the kids that it wouldn't matter.

Elke squeezed past him, carrying a soup tureen filled with beef stew, and his mouth watered at the fragrant scent. He set Beth down and snagged Ryan on the shoulder just as the boy reached out to snitch a square of corn bread. "You heard your sister. Let's wash up."

"You snuck a cookie."

"You're right. Sorry that I was a bad example."

Ryan looked chastised and followed him out to the mud room where a bucket of fresh water and clean towels awaited them. The boy washed quickly and snatched a towel. Quinn dipped his hands then flicked the water on Ryan. He jerked his head and giggled. Ryan tossed the towel at Quinn and dashed into the kitchen before Quinn could get him again. Splashing had become a game between the two of them.

Quinn rinsed his hands and dried them then used the towel to clean the dust off his face. When he lowered the towel, he was surprised to see Sarah leaning against the doorjamb, watching him with a raised brow.

"Splashing again?"

He grinned and shrugged. "Ryan enjoys it. I'm for anything that keeps him from scowling."

"Thank you. I appreciate how you and the ranch hands have taken him under your wing. I know he has to be in the way at times."

Quinn tossed the towel toward a peg on the wall, not a little proud that it caught and stayed there. "Everyone has to start somewhere. But who would have thought riding lessons would thaw the boy so quickly. After my initial outburst when I first saw them, I wondered if I'd ever get on his good side."

Sarah's pretty lips pressed together. "Losing our pa was really hard on Ryan. And then our uncle was just plain cruel. I'd never have gone to him if I'd known how much he'd changed. When I was a child, he was a fun man to be around."

"People change. Adversity can make a person cold and hard while others learn from their problems and get stronger." Somehow he knew Sarah was a survivor. Even though she'd been forced into a marriage she hadn't wanted, she'd never once treated him with scorn. She'd just accepted things for what they were and had gone about making things easier for Grandma and Elke.

A rosy stain covered her cheeks as he continued to stare. His stomach twittered as if a moth had found its way in there. Finally, Sarah dropped her gaze.

"I want you to know how much I appreciate you taking us in." She fiddled with the edge of her apron then looked up. "I'm sorry I didn't tell you about Ryan and Beth before we were married. That wasn't fair to you. I was afraid—"

Quinn grabbed her hand, surprised at its softness. "I know why you didn't tell me. I'll admit I was angry at first. I don't like surprises, but you did what was necessary to protect your siblings. That's something I know a lot about."

Sarah cocked her head and smiled. "Yes, I'm sure it is. Your grandma has told me how you helped raise your brother and sister."

That was a fact that most everyone knew, but when his wife said it with pride in her voice, embarrassment warmed his neck. His stomach gurgled.

Sarah grinned. "Hungry, huh?" She tugged him through the kitchen, dropping his hand just before they entered the dining room.

Quinn watched her glide toward her chair. Comfortable chatter filled the room as his wife took her seat. He no longer regretted marrying her—but he was fast coming to regret making his marriage a business arrangement.

nine

"Come closer and watch me, Ryan." Holding two new horse-shoes, the boy approached cautiously on Quinn's right. He lifted the mare's rear hoof between his legs and held up a tool. "This is a hoof pick. It's used to scrape out packed dirt, manure, and small stones from a horse's hoof."

Quinn cleaned the hoof and removed the old shoe. Ryan watched with something that looked like admiration on his face. "Hand me those nippers. You use them to trim the hoof wall." He quickly trimmed the hoof and used a rasp from his back pocket to smooth it out.

"I've already sized the shoes for this mare, so all that's left is to put on the new one." Ryan handed him a shoe, and Quinn tapped it on with a nailing hammer.

"What about the nail points sticking through the shoe?" Ryan asked as he bent closer, blocking the light.

"Clinch the nails—bend the ends—to keep the shoe from coming off. After that, smooth things with the rasp, and then you get to do that three more times." He dropped the mare's hoof, patted her rump, and rubbed his lower back. Ryan picked up the old shoe and examined it.

Quinn smiled and lightly squeezed the boy's shoulder. At least Ryan was no longer flinching whenever he touched him. Since acquiring a new family, Quinn had chosen chores that kept him closer to home. For someone who'd been a loner for so long, it was a big change. He bent and lodged the horse's front hoof between his legs, dug out a stone, and grated down the hoof. "Hand me the rasp again."

Ryan stood beside him watching each thing he did. Adam

had never been so interested in ranching. He'd done what had to be done but would slip off and draw pictures if their pa didn't keep a close eye on him. Ryan wanted to learn everything. He'd probably asked Quinn a hundred questions. With the new shoe nailed on, he lowered the hoof and patted the mare again. Why couldn't women be so easy to handle? "See, it's simple."

"Maybe to you." Ryan shrugged.

"It will be to you one day, too, after you've shod a few dozen horses."

He finished the last two hooves and then let the boy lead the horse into the corral and release her. Ryan was a quick learner. His coloring and features hardly resembled his big sister, except for those brilliant blue eyes they all had.

The odor of cattle hung on the cool breeze, reminding him of all the chores that needed doing. Fences needed mending. This spring's crop of calves still needed to be branded. His wife needed a real husband.

He shook his head, leaned on the corral, and lifted his foot to the first rail. Had it been a mistake to marry Sarah? Weren't she and the kids much better off?

Ryan closed the gate and mirrored his stance but remained silent. Quinn's thoughts veered to Sarah and how she had insisted he sleep on the bed. Ever since their second night together, she'd dressed in her nightgown before he'd come in and had slept on the sofa, wrapped up in a quilt. Sure, he was resting better than when he'd been on the floor, but the guilt was driving him crazy. She should take the bed, but she was too stubborn. What would she do if he picked her up in her sleep and put her in it? He grinned, but then realized that would mean he'd be sleeping on the floor again. He shook his head. There was no easy answer.

A squeal sounded from near the house, and the mare nickered and turned her head toward the noise. Quinn looked over his shoulder and saw Beth run around the side of the house. He pushed away from the railing and moved toward her. Was she hurt? Scared?

Sarah followed, laughing, and Quinn's bunched up muscles relaxed. She growled and lifted up her skirt and ran after her sister. "I'm gonna get you."

"Nuh-uh." Beth spotted him and ran in his direction. "Save me, Quinn! Don't let the mean old bear eat me."

Quinn reached out and caught Beth as she lunged for him. He spun her around then held her against his chest. "I'll protect you from that mean ol' critter."

Beth giggled and looked at her sister.

Sarah halted a few feet from him, her chest heaving. Her cheeks were a rosy red. "Looks like you've got my dinner, cowboy."

"Yep."

"What's a poor bear gonna do?"

Ryan slipped up beside Quinn, staring at his sisters as if they'd gone loco.

"Eat Ryan." Beth pointed at her brother, who peered back with interest.

Sarah's eyes gleamed, and she tiptoed toward Ryan with her hands making bear claws. A smile tugged at the somber boy's lips. "She can't catch me." He dashed toward the barn with Sarah close on his heels.

"C'mon, Quinn," Beth squealed and bounced in his arms. "We gotta save Ryan."

Grinning, Quinn jogged toward the barn. Inside, Sarah tackled her brother, and both landed in a pile of fresh hay that was ready to be forked into the clean stalls. Ryan laughed as Sarah tickled him.

"Let me down." Beth kicked, and he set her on the ground. The little girl dove on top of her sister.

Quinn leaned one arm on a stall gate, wishing he had the

freedom to jump in and play with them. They reminded him of the days when his family still lived in Texas. When he was a boy and had horsed around with Adam and Anna—before they moved here and their father died and everything changed. He missed those carefree days. Maybe one day he'd feel comfortable enough to wrestle with Sarah and the kids like that.

But then Sarah and the kids weren't staying.

Ryan jumped up and dashed past Quinn with Beth on his heels. Quinn grinned at the two, who more resembled scarecrows with all that hay in their hair than children. Chuckling, Sarah sat up and plucked stems from the cuff and pocket of one of Anna's old dresses. She rested her arms on her knees, a wide grin on her face.

"It's so good to see them laughing again," Sarah said. "I have you to thank for that."

Quinn pushed away from the stall and strode toward her. He reached out his hand, and she glanced up. After a moment she placed her hand in his, and he drew her to her feet. Sprigs of hay stuck out from his wife's dark hair, and her thick braid rested over her shoulder, hanging down the front of her dress. He couldn't help grinning.

"What's so funny?"

He may be just a rancher, but he knew better than to answer that question. He lifted a hand and pulled out a stem near her ear. Then another off of the top of her head. His wife swallowed. Did he affect her like she did him? He'd never been drawn to a woman before. Never allowed himself to get close enough to get to know one. And now he was married. Sort of.

His wife had filled out a little in the week that she'd been at the Rocking M. Her cheeks were rosy, and she'd lost that wary look. She was filling a place in his heart that he hadn't known was empty.

He'd been lonely but hadn't noticed until Sarah and the kids arrived. He'd worked hard all day and spent his evenings doing bookkeeping or reading up on cattle breeding or diseases. He hadn't had time to be lonely. And now that Sarah was here, he was lonelier than ever. As much as he didn't want to admit it, he wanted her to care for him—not because he'd provided her family with a home and food, but because she saw something in him worth desiring.

His wife nibbled on her bottom lip. Quinn plucked a stem of hay from the top of her head and ran his hand down her soft hair. It was black as a raven's wing. Her lightly tanned skin seemed fairer than it actually was in the shadows of the barn. Her questioning sky blue eyes peered up at him.

His breath caught in his throat as he thought about kissing her. Would she welcome his affection? It was unwise to be thinking such thoughts. She would leave him one day. But he couldn't help leaning toward her. She lifted her face up to his.

A piercing scream echoed behind him, and Quinn spun around. Beth ran toward him with Ryan right behind her. "Save me again, Quinn!"

Beth dashed behind him and wrapped her arms around his waist. Disappointment soared through him at the missed kiss.

But maybe the little girl had saved *him*. Saved him from making a big mistake.

❧

Martha lifted a linen baby gown from the top of the trunk and handed it to Sarah. "This was Adam's. He and Anna were so tiny when they were born, it's a miracle they survived. Even though she was just married, Anna took her matching gown and some other baby things with her when she moved to Brett's ranch, hoping it wouldn't be long before she was with child."

Beth leaned against Sarah's arm and fingered the thin fabric.

"It's small enough to fit a dolly."

"Go get your doll and let's see if it does." Grandma smiled and ran her hand over the little girl's head.

Beth glanced up at Sarah, her eyes shimmering with unshed tears. Sarah pressed her sister against her side as the scent of smoke and the vision of a burned home still smoldering assaulted her. Just when she thought she was over her grief, it washed over her again like a spring flash flood.

"Beth doesn't have a doll anymore."

"It burned up in the fire like Mama and Papa." The girl's lower lip wobbled and a tear streaked down her cheek.

"I'm sorry, dear." Martha pressed her lips together, as if she, too, struggled not to give way to tears. "We'll just have to make a new doll. I have a box of scraps in my room. Would you like to come and look at them after we finish here and see if you can find something that would make a nice doll?"

"Can Sarah come, too?" Beth looked back and forth between the two women.

"Of course she can." Quinn's grandmother dug further down in the trunk and pulled out two folded garments. She shook out a blue calico and held it up to Beth. "It's a bit big, but we can alter it to fit you."

Beth's eyes lit up. "Look, Sissy, Grandma's giving me another new dress."

Sarah's gaze caught Martha's, and a soft smile flitted on the older woman's lips. "It's been a long while since a child has called me Grandma. It sounds good to these old ears."

"Why don't you try on the dress, Beth? Then we can pin it up."

Beth quickly shed her old garment and slipped the new one over her head. Martha got her pin cushion, and Sarah pinned up the sides of the garment while Martha measured.

"Now the second one." Martha shook out a brown calico with a pinafore that would make a sturdy play garment.

Beth shed the blue dress and pulled on the second. She stood on one foot and then the other.

"You remind me of Anna at your age. The poor child hated trying on clothes. She'd much rather be out riding a horse or chasing cattle."

Beth scratched her neck where the dress pressed against her throat. "Quinn's gonna teach me to ride like he did Ryan."

Martha laid the blue garment on Sarah's bed. "That's a good thing to know, even for women and girls. I used to help my husband with roundup back when we lived in Texas, and Anna helped here."

Sarah smiled as she measured the second dress. "I think this one will be fine in the side. I'll take the hem up a little and have it ready for you to wear tomorrow."

Beth clapped her hands. "Goodie. Can I go play with the blocks now?"

Sarah buttoned up the back of Beth's faded calico and hugged her sister. "Yes, you may. Just stay on the porch. If you want to go see the animals or something else, you come and get me first. All right?"

Beth nodded and skipped out of the room. A warm sensation filled Sarah's chest. Quinn had made her sister's happiness possible. He may have had second thoughts about making their marriage real, but the result for her siblings had been the same. Both were happier than they'd been since the fire.

Martha held a knitted baby blanket against her chest. "I hope to be able to use this again one day soon."

Her sly smile sent a shaft of guilt spearing through Sarah. How could she tell this sweet woman that there wouldn't be any children from her marriage? That her husband wanted a business arrangement and would send her packing once Martha was gone?

She couldn't. Sarah forced a smile. "Maybe one day."

"Adam's little Jonathon is a cherub. He's got his father's coloring, much like your blue eyes and dark hair. Adam always hated that he didn't look much like Quinn and Anna, even though he was Anna's twin." Martha seemed to stare off in the distance, as if she were looking right at Adam. She blinked and turned back to Sarah, an ornery smile tilting her lips. "I certainly hope to see Anna's and Quinn's children before I leave this world."

Sarah patted Martha's arm. She didn't want to give the woman false hope, but surely it wouldn't be long before Anna had a baby. "I'm sure you will."

She picked up the scissors from Martha's sewing basket and carried the dress to the sofa. She flipped the garment inside out and snipped the threads on the side seams.

If only she could tell Martha the truth. That her marriage was a lie. She peeked over her shoulder at the woman she was quickly growing to love. Martha was kind and generous, opening her home and her heart to Sarah and the children. She'd never asked how Sarah had come to marry her grandson, but rather just seemed happy that she had.

Sarah heaved a sigh. Everything here was perfect. The home was rugged but had most everything they needed. Elke was a good cook, and they were getting used to eating all the German specialties the woman enjoyed making. Ryan had even started eating sauerkraut.

Quinn ran the ranch with expertise. He worked hard and was gone nearly all day. Most times they didn't see him for the noon meal because he was out on the range tending the cattle. Now that Ryan was riding well, he often accompanied Quinn at least half of the day. The exhausted boy was little trouble and fell asleep most nights on top of his bed with his clothes still on.

The top of the trunk thunked as Martha closed it, and

Sarah jumped, stabbing her finger with a pin. She sucked the blood off so that it wouldn't stain the fabric. She stared at the cold fireplace that took up nearly the whole wall. The room held the scent of wood smoke and furniture wax, giving it a cozy, homey feel.

Martha ambled over and sat beside Sarah, holding the brown dress. She picked up the scissors lying on the couch between them and snipped the threads that secured the hem. "Is everything all right between you and Quinn? I mean, I'm sure you and he didn't marry for love, since you'd never met before you were married, but are you happy here?"

"Oh yes. I love it here." Sarah couldn't tell the whole story, but that much was true. Life at her uncle's shack had been a daily struggle to survive. She had to hunt for food because he said she owed him. Then she had to clean and cook the meat, if she was fortunate enough to even kill something.

"I'm glad. I'll admit I was quite surprised when my grandson came home with you and the children, but you've been a delight and pulled me out of my grieving."

Sarah laid her hand over Martha's. "I'm sorry about your daughter. I wish I could have met her."

"Parents shouldn't outlive their children." Martha rested her hands in her lap. "Things were very difficult when Quinn's father died, and my grandson had to grow up overnight. He had a ranch to run, a grieving mother to help, and twin siblings who needed guidance. He's a good man."

Sarah nodded, thinking again how Quinn had been willing to marry her even though he didn't know for sure if she was an outlaw. Not many men would have taken that risk. She'd always be grateful that he most likely saved her brother's and sister's lives.

"He used to go to church each Sunday, but after his pa died, it was as if something in him closed off. He didn't want to feel anymore."

"Why are you telling me this?"

"Because I want you to understand him. To know that he's a good man who has endured a lot of pain and is afraid to open up. You, my dear, are the only person I think who can get him to do so."

Sarah watched Martha return to her sewing. The older woman had no idea of the burden that she'd just dumped on Sarah. If her marriage to Quinn was a love-match, then maybe she could help him, but she was just a fake wife. One to keep his grandma from ordering another mail-order bride.

She thought of all she'd lost, and the pain of losing this home hit full force. How long would they be here? A few months? A few years?

Long enough for the children to get settled. Long enough that leaving here would cause them great disappointment.

I can't think about that day, Lord. It takes more energy than I have. Help me to make things easier for Martha. Keep her healthy and happy, and show me how to make my husband fall in love with me.

Just how did a woman go about making that happen?

ten

"You missed a spot." Sarah pared the peeling off the potato in one long swirl.

"Where?" Beth turned a potato over in her hand, her palm effectively covering the last of the peeling.

Sarah lifted her sister's thumb. "Right there. It's hiding from you."

Beth giggled and cut off the last spot.

Sarah leaned her head back against the rocker. Sitting on the porch watching the birds flittering on the railings or the men working a new horse in the corral helped pass the time while she did monotonous chores. A comfortable breeze tugged at her skirt and cooled her legs. Off to her left, two magpies bickered and flapped their wings.

Russet buttes surrounded the cozy valley, forming a natural shelter from the heavy winds that sometimes threatened to blow away anything not tied down. Clean sheets snapped on the line, absorbing the fresh scent created only by the sun and wind. The few trees in the area followed the creek line nearly a quarter of a mile away, offering shade to those willing to take the time to walk down there. Maybe she should take the children to play in the water one afternoon while the temperatures were warm.

Sarah sighed and picked up another potato. If only she could relax and enjoy the peaceful setting, but Quinn's words still haunted her. She couldn't let herself get attached to this place, no matter how comfortable it was. Homes were temporary. How many times had her parents moved before settling on the farm? Fire destroyed homes. People destroyed homes. As long as she and the children were together, that was where home was.

Sarah lifted her face to the breeze and sniffed. A hint of something filled the air, so unlike the stench of sugar beets. Sage, maybe.

A rider appeared at the top of the hill, following the trail she and Quinn had taken from town. She shaded her eyes as he drew closer. The roan horse moved into a trot, and Sarah's heart lurched. Uncle Harlan owned a roan gelding. Had he found them already?

Ryan was safe out on the range somewhere with Quinn. She set three finished spuds in Beth's bowl, her hand shaking so badly that she dropped one.

"I'll get it." Beth jumped up and set her smaller bowl in the rocker next to Sarah's.

"Why don't you go inside and wash that potato and give the finished ones to Elke so she can put them to soak. We don't want them turning brown before we're ready to use them."

She glanced at the rider again and let out a relieved sigh. Now that the man was closer, she could tell he was too thin to be her uncle. *Thank you, Lord.*

He rode toward the house at a comfortable lope, looking too relaxed to be someone bringing trouble. He stopped his horse in front of her and tipped his hat, gazing at her with a curious, but friendly stare. Had he heard that Quinn had married a jailbird?

"*Guten tag.* I am Howard Heinrich. I am owner of the ranch south of here."

Sarah nodded and smiled at his thick German accent, which sounded similar to Elke's. "I'm Quinn's wife, Sarah McFarland."

The man grinned, revealing yellowed teeth. "I heard about you when I was in the town. Quite a story that is."

Sarah narrowed her eyes, not sure what he wanted.

"I do not mean harm. I bring mail. Neighbors here do that for one another." He reached behind him, pulled a small packet from his saddlebags, and thumbed through the letters. He handed three to Sarah.

"Would you like something to drink?" It was the least she could offer after his kindness.

"*Danke,* Frau McFarland, but I wish to get home before the dark." He tipped his hat and clucked out the side of his mouth to his horse. He reached the top of the hill and disappeared down the other side before the dust settled on the trail.

Sarah glanced at the mail. Two letters were for Quinn and one for his grandmother. She found Martha in the kitchen, rolling buns for supper.

"You've got a letter." Sarah held it while Martha wiped her hands on her apron.

"Mr. Heinrich must have stopped by." She smiled and squinted then pushed her spectacles up her nose as she took the letter from Sarah. She slit the envelope with a knife and unfolded a single sheet of paper. "It's from my husband's brother."

Sarah hoped the note brought good news but couldn't help wondering how many more relatives the family had that she didn't know about.

"John is coming for a visit and is bringing Tom and Florinda Phillips with him." Martha laid the letter on the table next to a bowl of dough. "They come most every year to get away from the heat of the city. Of course, half the time it's just as hot here as in Chicago."

"When will they be arriving?" Sarah had barely gotten used to living on the Rocking M and now visitors were coming. Would they ask how she and Quinn met?

Martha glanced at the note again. "Oh, dear. They'll be

here next week. There's so much to do."

"The children and I will help get things ready." Sarah patted Martha's shoulder, happy to do whatever she could to help. She didn't want her to stress over this sudden news and take to her bed, even though she hadn't been in bed a single day since they'd arrived. Sarah suspected the illness Quinn had mentioned was actually Martha grieving over the loss of her daughter, and her Bismarck home and friends. Sarah remembered the three babes her mother had lost before Beth and Ryan had been born. After each loss, her mother had been downhearted and had barely eaten for a long while. Grieving was a process that men didn't have the time or patience for and often didn't understand. "Where should I put these letters for Quinn?"

"On his desk in the parlor. I need to make a list of everything we'll have to do before John comes." Martha stared off as if deep in thought. Sarah tapped the other two letters against her hand.

Beth walked through the mud room, lugging a bucket with two inches of water with Elke following close behind her. "Elke helped me get water, and I'm gonna wash the 'tatoes, Sissy."

"That's being a good helper." Sarah smiled. Her sister probably had more water running down the front of her dress than in the bucket. She needed to make Beth an apron to protect her new dresses.

As Elke passed by, Sarah lightly touched her arm and leaned toward her. "Thank you for letting Beth help. I realize it makes more work for you."

The shy, fair-haired woman with pale blue eyes kept her head down, but a soft smile graced her lips. "I like *kinder*, Frau McFarland. I was oldest of nine."

"Nine?" Sarah regretted her impulsive response, but it didn't seem to bother the quiet cook.

"*Ja*, we have big family." Elke helped Beth onto a chair and then poured a small amount of water into a basin. Beth washed the potatoes and then dropped them into the bucket of water.

Sarah walked through the dining area and into the parlor, trying to imagine what it would be like to have been raised in such a large family. Maybe that was why Elke wasn't married. The woman had to be in her early thirties. Maybe she liked children—as long as they weren't hers.

She placed the letters on Quinn's desk, noting the neatness of the few items arranged on it. The only thing even partly messy was an open book. She glanced down to see what her husband had been reading and wrinkled her nose at the chapter heading. "New Methods in Castrating Cattle."

Martha followed her into the parlor and stared up at a family portrait on the wall. Sarah recognized the gangly adolescent as Quinn. A handsome man stood behind a blond woman sitting in a chair. Adam and Anna stood in front of their older brother. Anna's light-colored hair matched Quinn's and their mother's, while Adam's was dark like his father's.

"Quinn's father dreamed of owning a ranch where city folk could visit and find rest from the hectic life of the big towns. Ian received an inheritance from a wealthy uncle who lived in Ireland. He was the only heir and used the money to buy this ranch and to move his family here." She looked down and fiddled with the hem of her apron. "I didn't want them to leave Texas, but there been had a long drought. Times were tough, and there were still some problems with Indians sneaking across the Red River from Indian Territory and raiding ranches."

Sarah lifted her brows. Had Martha ever battled Indians? Ever shot one to protect her family? She stared at the portrait, trying to see a resemblance between Martha and her daughter.

"Ellen was very pretty."

"Yes. She was a sweet woman who endured a hard life. Things up here weren't much easier than they'd been in Texas." She motioned toward the horsehair sofa and both women sat.

"You're a McFarland now. I doubt Quinn will tell you about his family history, but you ought to know. His father built this wonderful home, and things were going well. They were building up their herd by selling off longhorns and purchasing hardy cattle that fared better in the colder winters we have. Then Ian died in a tragic accident."

"What happened?" Sarah shivered as a vision of the fire seared her memory. She and her husband had suffered similar losses.

"He was returning from town with a wagon of supplies and a bad storm set in while he was gone. His wagon wheels slipped on the ice—we think—and the wagon went off a cliff. Thank the good Lord none of the children were with him."

Sarah laid her hand over Martha's. "I'm sorry."

"It was a long time ago, but Quinn's life changed that day. He went from being a fairly responsible adolescent who liked to hunt and fish to helping raise the twins and being in charge of the ranch. I think he's always felt that he failed his father by not opening the ranch up to city folk, other than family and a few cattlemen who come occasionally. You can see why I'm hoping you and he will be very happy together. He desperately needs some happiness in his life."

"I suppose that's why this home has so many bedrooms." Sarah wanted to encourage Martha, but she wouldn't give her false hopes about her marriage.

Martha nodded. "Yes. We can put John and Mr. Phillips in that empty room with the two beds. I'm afraid we'll need to move Beth into Ryan's room as long as the company is here. Do you think that will be all right? They're both still young enough to sleep together."

"It will be fine. We all shared a—" She caught herself before saying mat. She didn't want Martha to know they'd slept on buffalo skins on the hard floor of her uncle's shack. She didn't need the woman's pity. "We slept together for a time after my parents died."

"That will make things easier. We can put Florinda in Anna's old room."

"Florinda?"

Martha's lips pulled into a tight grimace. "Yes, she's Tom Phillips's daughter and usually accompanies him when he comes to visit. He's a well-known beef supplier and buys cattle from Quinn and then ships them to a Chicago slaughterhouse that he owns. Florinda has always been a bit. . .flighty. I think the only reason she comes is because of Qui—" Martha suddenly looked as if she'd swallowed a fly. "Well, never mind."

Because of Quinn. That's what she'd almost said. Sarah was certain of it. Did this Florinda have designs on Quinn? Sarah wondered why a city woman would want to visit such an isolated ranch. Surely she would be bored here, but then she must like it if she'd been here before. Or maybe she just liked Quinn. What would Florinda do when she learned he was now married?

The idea of another woman attracted to her handsome husband made Sarah's stomach swirl as if she'd downed a glass of sour milk. Had Quinn been attracted to their guest? If so, why did he marry Sarah? Would she have to do battle to keep the husband who already wanted to be rid of her?

❧

"They're coming! I see them." Beth ran through the open front door, her braids flying behind her.

Ryan tugged at the collar of his new white shirt. "I don't see why we have to wear our fancy clothes just 'cause company's coming?" He fidgeted on the steps.

Sarah wished she'd been able to purchase new shoes for him and Beth, but at least Martha had insisted they draw an outline of the children's feet, so Quinn could drop it off at the mercantile. Next time someone went into town, the new shoes, ordered from a cobbler in Dickinson, should be waiting.

Martha hurried through the parlor in the tan and gold church dress that Sarah had ironed for her the day before. The older woman, eager to see her husband's younger brother, looked excited, even vibrant, and not a bit sick. Sarah mumbled a thank-you to God for that.

She smoothed down the front of her dress, glad that she was able to complete the dark blue calico before their guests arrived. Her hands trembled. She'd worked herself into a tizzy the past few days worrying about Florinda Phillips. So what if the woman had designs on Quinn? What could she do now that he was married?

Sarah took a deep breath. She knew she shouldn't worry so. God had provided this home and family to care for them, and He would work out their future.

Beth bounced up and down, and Sarah rested her hand on the girl's shoulder. "Settle down. Those folks aren't coming to see us." She couldn't understand why Beth was so excited. Maybe it had to do with the cookies they would be serving once their guests had settled in.

Quinn guided a handsome black surrey with a folded leather top into the yard, pulled by one of the prettiest horses Sarah had seen. She couldn't help thinking how she had arrived on an old buckboard filled with supplies. Two men sat in the backseat, but Sarah's gaze was drawn to the beautiful woman in the front, leaning against Quinn's shoulder. Her neatly styled blond hair was covered by a small hat that held no purpose other than decoration. Her frilly lavender dress looked out of place against the browns and greens of the valley.

"Whoa, Charlie. Hold up, boy." Quinn hopped down, hurried around to the other side of the buggy, and offered his hand to Florinda. The woman gave him a coy smile then set her hands on top of his shoulders, forcing him to take hold of her thin waist and lift her down. She giggled and took his arm, ignoring everyone on the porch as she gazed longingly at Sarah's husband.

Sarah clenched her teeth. How could she endure this preening woman for two full weeks? Quinn glanced at her, and she lifted one brow and stared back. He looked down, as if watching the steps to make sure he didn't trip—steps he dashed up and down a dozen times each day.

The two men climbed out of the buggy. A tall, thin man looked around the ranch, but the shorter, balding man, who looked twenty years older than the other man, made a beeline for Martha.

"Oh, John. I can't believe you're actually here." Martha held out her arms.

He hurried up the stairs as soon as Florinda's skirts had cleared them and wrapped his arms around the older woman. "I was so sorry to hear about Ellen. I would have come if I hadn't been in New York."

Martha patted his chest. "It's all right. She was probably buried before you even received our telegram."

"How are you doing?" he asked.

"Fine. Much better now that I've moved to the ranch. I needed to be with family."

Florinda narrowed her eyes and curled her lip as she regarded Sarah. Her hazel gaze darted from Beth to Ryan before settling, adoringly, back on Quinn. Sarah couldn't help wondering if Miss Phillips thought they were the hired help.

Mr. Phillips joined them on the porch and stood beside his daughter. He had kind gray eyes, and a thick head of light brown hair. He stood about three inches shorter than Quinn.

Sarah's husband wriggled his arm away from Florinda's and stepped toward Martha. "You remember my grandmother, Martha Miles. You two met three or four years ago in Bismarck."

Florinda's smile would have won a grinning contest, if there were such a thing. "How nice to see you again." She gently shook Martha's hand.

"It's a pleasure to have you visit the Rocking M."

"Yes, well. . .thank you." Florinda's gaze flitted over the front of the house, and Sarah felt like the woman would rather be just about anywhere except an isolated ranch in the Badlands.

Quinn crossed over to stand beside Sarah. He cast a quick glance her way and cleared his throat. "Uncle John, Mr. Phillips, Florinda, I'd like to introduce my. . .wife, Sarah."

Sarah couldn't help taking a small pleasure in the way Florinda's brows shot up. At the same time she hadn't missed how Quinn had hem-hawed when he introduced her. Was he ashamed of her?

"Well now, this is a surprise. Congratulations, my boy." Uncle John slapped Quinn on the shoulder and gave him a rough hug. "It's about time you married."

He turned to Sarah. "Welcome to the family." Before she could shake his hand, he engulfed her in a bear hug, making Sarah feel loved and accepted. She already liked the man. "And are these your children?"

Martha slapped her brother-in-law on the arm. "Oh for heaven's sake, John, she's far too young to have children that age. They are her siblings, Ryan and Beth."

With introductions completed, Uncle John followed Martha and Mr. Phillips inside. Florinda seemed to have gathered her composure and grasped hold of Quinn's left arm, giving Sarah a derisive glare. Quinn glanced from Sarah to Florinda as if unsure what to do. He shifted his feet, looking uncomfortable with Florinda's overt attention. Sarah wasn't about to let the woman get away with such an action, and she took hold of Quinn's right arm.

"Will you please escort us into the house, *husband*?" If Quinn seemed surprised at her overly emphasized spousal reference, he didn't show it.

Sarah clung to him, ready to do battle for the man who didn't want her. Maybe she just needed to prove to the flirty woman that Quinn belonged to her, even if he didn't realize it yet.

eleven

Sarah set the sugar bowl on the table and then stopped in front of the open window. She allowed the wind to cool her body, hot from helping Elke in the kitchen, while she struggled to calm her emotions, equally as steamy. Fortunately, this evening's breeze was from the north and not the south, where the cattle were currently grazing. She took several deep breaths and then took her seat between Quinn and Beth. Florinda sat across from them, alternating glares at Sarah with cocked-head smiles at Quinn. Did the woman not realize how obvious her flirtations were?

Learning that Quinn was married and unavailable seemed to have no effect on Miss Phillips. Sarah had worked to catch the eye of a few boys back during her school days, but this was different. What could Florinda hope to gain?

A cold shiver snaked up Sarah's spine. What if Florinda discouraged her father from buying cattle from Quinn if he didn't shower her with attention? Surely Mr. Phillips wouldn't allow something so petty to keep him from making a wise business decision.

"I thought we'd ride out and look at the cattle tomorrow, if that's all right with you two. The weather's not too hot yet, so it shouldn't be a hardship for you city slickers." Quinn grinned at the men and then sipped his coffee.

"Perhaps they would like a day to rest from their travels," Martha said.

Elke set a platter heaping with fried chicken on the table. Sarah's mouth watered as she eyed the golden crust. She knew it was tasty, because she'd sampled the little crispies that had fallen off as Elke took the chicken from the skillet. At least their nauseating guest hadn't affected her appetite. She couldn't help grinning the next time Florinda glared at her.

"I feel fine and would like to see the cattle tomorrow. How about you, John?" Mr. Phillips looked at his friend.

"Sounds good to me as long as it doesn't rain."

At Martha's request, John said a quick prayer, and the food was passed. Florinda took one chicken leg and a tablespoon of potatoes, minus the gravy, and green peas. Sarah didn't let the other woman's puny appetite affect her and filled her plate. She was famished. She'd worked hard all day preparing the rooms, cleaning house, and cooking.

While the men talked weather and cattle prices, Martha attempted to engage Miss Phillips in conversation. "What have you been doing with yourself lately, Florinda?"

Ryan, sitting to Miss Phillips's left, finished off a thigh and licked his fingers with a smack. Sarah lifted her brows at him, and he ducked his head and retrieved his napkin from the floor where it had fallen.

Miss Phillips scowled at the boy as she dabbed her lips with her cloth napkin. Her expression softened when she turned her gaze on Martha. "Oh, the usual. Last year I completed finishing school at Miss Muriel Murdock's Academy for Fine Ladies. We learned culture and sophistication." She lifted her nose and looked at Sarah's plate. "Something you most likely know nothing about."

Martha cleared her throat, obviously displeased with the comment. Sarah nearly bit clear through the chicken bone. She glanced at Quinn who was engrossed in his conversation and completely missed how she had been insulted.

"Some people have to work for a living and can't go to those fancy schools." Ryan squinted at Florinda; his lips looked as if he'd sucked on a lemon.

Sarah wanted to run over and hug her brother for defending her, but she stayed in her chair and took a bite of potatoes—with plenty of gravy.

"Well, things are different out West." Martha took a sip of buttermilk. "Most young ladies around here marry early. People don't have money for such luxuries as finishing school. You're a fortunate girl to have been able to attend such a fine academy." Martha caught Sarah's eye and smiled at her as if letting her know she understood how Florinda irritated her.

Sarah endured the rest of the meal, grateful to leave when it was time to help the children get ready for bed. Florinda smirked as Sarah stood, and Sarah didn't take time to analyze the crazy thought that sprinted across her mind, but she leaned over and kissed Quinn on the cheek, all the time looking at Florinda. The line in the sand had been drawn.

Quinn jerked around and looked at Sarah with confused eyes. She leaned her arm across his shoulders, her soft cheek rubbing against his bristly one. "If you'll excuse me for a moment, I'm just going to put the children in bed. I'll be right back, so don't you go anywhere."

One of his brows lifted, but he quickly schooled his expression as if he was onto her. "I'll be right here waiting." He grinned and winked as she straightened, sending her stomach into spasms. Maybe she had eaten too much.

Martha and the men chuckled. Florinda's perpetual scowl deepened. Feeling lighter than she had all day, Sarah took Beth's hand and helped the yawning girl out of her chair. "Come along, Ryan."

Her brother snagged another biscuit and stood. "'Scuse me," he mumbled. He shoved the bread into his mouth and walked around the table.

Sarah considered how being so close to Quinn had affected her. He smelled fresh, having bathed in the creek before going to town to fetch their guests. He had a scent all his own, a manly one that never failed to stir her whenever he came near. His dark blond hair, which was normally covered with his western hat, swirled in appealing curls. His forehead was a shade lighter than the rest of his tanned face. She'd tried not to like him too much, but he was a good, kind man. He worked hard, cared for his grandmother—even loved Martha enough to marry a woman he didn't know just to make her happy. At least that's what Sarah had decided was the reason.

She sighed as she walked into Beth's room. Having to stake her claim on her husband was exhausting. Still, there was something exciting about shamelessly cuddling him like she had. She couldn't help smiling. Maybe she'd just have to kiss him again.

A plan formed in her mind. If she laid claim to Quinn and showed more affection, maybe he'd start liking her more. What could it hurt?

❧

Quinn led three horses out of the barn and looped their reins over the hitching post in front of the house. John and Tom stood on the porch talking with Martha and Florinda. Quinn double-checked his rifle, making sure it was loaded. He didn't expect trouble, but he would be prepared just in case.

Florinda looked past her father, and her face lit up when she saw Quinn. He pursed his lips. He'd never liked her blatant attention and always wondered what game she was playing. Every time she visited the Rocking M, she would sidle up close and try to get him to notice her. Oh, sure she was pretty, if you liked fancified women. Her blond hair reminded him of his mother's, and her clothing resembled something Mariah, his sister-in-law who was from Chicago, might wear. But that was the only way Florinda was similar to the other women.

Instead of joining them on the porch, he checked the saddles on each of the horses, even though he knew they were fine. A shadow darkened the ground behind the horses, and Quinn sighed. Looks like there was no avoiding Miss Phillips this morning. At least they'd be gone all day.

Quinn glanced up and saw Sarah standing four feet behind the horses with a bundle in her arms. A shy smile graced her lips, and he remembered again how she'd kissed him the evening before. He'd be as stupid as a prairie dog to not realize what she was doing, but the thing that surprised him was how much he liked her attention. He'd never had a woman cuddle up to him, other than one of his relatives and Florinda, and that was not the same thing. Not even close.

Sarah's cheeks turned red, and he realized he'd been staring. He patted the horses' rumps as he walked between two of them toward his wife.

"Elke packed a lunch for you men. I thought I'd bring it to you so she wouldn't have to. She's busy in the kitchen." Sarah studied the ground then looked toward the porch. Her thin brows dipped down, and she refocused on him.

"Thanks. We'll appreciate the food later on." He took the bundle and tied it over his saddle horn then walked back to Sarah. Florinda glided down the steps and aimed for them.

Something like panic crossed Sarah's face, and she visibly swallowed and stepped closer to him. His heart thumped at her nearness. He wasn't sure what had gotten into her last night at dinner, but he liked it. Whatever it was hadn't carried over to their bedroom, though. By the time he finished talking with the men and had retired, she was sound asleep on the settee with a quilt wrapped tight around her. He'd watched her for a few minutes before taking off his boots. In her sleep, she looked younger, innocent. A desire to protect her surged up through him with the speed of a barn fire.

She reached out and fiddled with a button on his chest. He took a deep breath and stood still. "Have a good day, and come back safely." A soft smile pulled at her lips, and she peeked up at him as if she had more on her mind. Sarah stood on her tiptoes, leaning closer to him. He bent down, and she placed a gentle kiss on his lips then awkwardly wrapped her arms around him in a hug. He squeezed back, shocked at the sensations racing through him.

He'd been a loner for so long that he hadn't realized how lonely he was. "You don't have to worry about Florinda," he murmured in her ear. "I tolerate her because I need her father's business."

Sarah's eyes widened, and a shy smile graced her lips. She nodded and darted away like a spooked bird. Florinda approached with her arms crossed and narrowed her eyes. Was she suspicious about his relationship with Sarah? What did it matter if she was?

"I was hoping to talk to you. Hoping that *we* could spend some time together." Florinda's expression softened, and she batted her lashes at him. "It's been so long since I last saw you."

"I'm a married man, Miss Phillips. I don't think it would be proper for me to escort you around the ranch like I have in the past."

"But—"

"You're free to walk around the ranch yard alone. Just don't venture farther than you can see the house." Quinn tipped his hat to her and mounted his horse. He knew Florinda would try to persuade him to change his mind if he gave her the chance. Even though his sister had volunteered in the past, his mother had always made him escort Florinda on walks whenever she visited, probably hoping he'd fall for the pretty gal. But she was too shallow for him, too obvious in her attentions, and someone like her would never be happy stuck on a ranch for months at a time. He'd thought the same thing about Sarah at first, but she seemed to love it here.

Quinn cleared his throat. The men laughed at something

his grandmother said and then they stomped down the steps and mounted their horses. Quinn glanced at Florinda, still standing where she'd been observing him and Sarah. Was she jealous?

He smiled at that thought. She'd never had competition for his attention before. He could imagine Florinda's shock if she knew the truth about his marriage. Her astonishment would only last a moment before it molded into smug superiority. Miss Phillips already looked down on Sarah, although he had no idea why.

Sarah was as sweet as the day was long. She treated his grandmother with kindness and respect, and Martha seemed much improved having Sarah around to help her and the children to pamper. Marrying her had been a wiser decision than he first realized. Too bad he'd wanted to keep things businesslike.

He rode up the hill and looked back over his shoulder to see if his wife was still outside. Sadly, she wasn't. Her sudden attempts at affection had been a pleasant surprise. Did she think if she treated him more like a husband that he'd let her stay after his grandmother was gone?

The idea sounded better and better.

"Which way, Quinn?" Uncle John stared at him with raised brows, and Quinn felt his neck warm as if the men could read his thoughts.

"Let's keep heading south. Just follow that trail." John and Tom rode ahead of him, and Quinn thought he heard one of them mumble, "Newlywed." He nudged his horse into a canter and passed the men.

He thought again how Sarah had pressed her hands against his chest as she leaned up to kiss him. His heart had pounded like he'd just run a mile-long race. He'd be lying if he said he hadn't liked her advances. Her cheek was so soft, and her lips warm.

But was Sarah's behavior simply an act for the sake of their visitors? To prove to Florinda that they were truly married?

He pressed his lips together. If that was the case, he would be sorely disappointed when his guests left.

twelve

Sarah stepped onto the porch and covered her eyes, looking for Ryan. The boy had wanted to ride with Quinn and the men, but Quinn had said no since they'd be discussing business. Her brother had stomped off to the barn, pouting. The tenseness in her shoulders relaxed when she saw him sitting on a bale of hay, just outside of the barn, mending tack with Claude. The old man had taken a shine to Ryan and had been a good influence on him.

Beth was in the kitchen helping Martha roll buns for supper. Florinda had retreated to her room after Quinn left. Sarah would love to know what conversation had passed between the two of them, but it mustn't have been pleasant since Miss Phillips had been puckered up like a prune when Quinn rode out. Sarah shook her head. How could any woman be so flirtatious with a married man? It was shameless and obviously a topic that had been overlooked at that fancy school.

She was thankful to have a few minutes to herself and headed to her bedroom to do the dusting. With company coming, she hadn't cleaned it, knowing no one would venture in there. At least she'd be away from Miss Phillips's scowls. She crossed through the empty parlor and into the hall.

Florinda sashayed out of her room, nearly colliding with Sarah. "Oh, it's you."

The woman had a way of getting under Sarah's skin worse than a chigger. She swallowed back her irritation, knowing the woman was Martha's guest. Sarah forced a congenial smile. "Was there something you needed?"

"Don't think you can fool me. I can tell there are no true feelings between you and Quinn." Florinda narrowed her eyes. "What were you? One of those forlorn mail-order brides? Quinn would never have married you if he'd seen you first."

Her words cut like a freshly sharpened knife. Sarah knew they stung now, but the pain would be stronger later, after she had time to consider them. She lifted her chin, wishing she were taller. "No. He saw me before we were married— more than once, in fact."

"Well, he must have been desperate. Not many women would want to be stuck in such a rustic place as this all winter."

"Then why are you so interested in *my* husband?"

Florinda laughed and waved her hand in the air. "Oh, you wouldn't understand. Quinn's a handsome man, and I've always been able to wrap him around my little finger."

Sarah stifled a gasp that tried to slip out. Surely that wasn't true. The stuffy heat of the dim, narrow hallway didn't help the situation. A rivulet of sweat trickled down her temple. Could it be possible that Quinn hid his true feelings for Florinda?

Florinda uttered a harsh laugh. "Quinn will never be satisfied with you. You're nothing but a tumbleweed bride— scrub brush plain. I've planned to marry Quinn ever since the time we met years ago at his grandparents' ranch in Texas, and I won't give him up without a fight."

Sarah straightened, almost looking Miss Phillips in the eye. "You're too late. Quinn is already married, and we're pledged to each other before God and the church." Quinn may not want her, but she'd never tell Florinda that. She'd do everything in her power to keep him. She had to—for the children's sake.

Miss Phillips waved her hand in the air like a fan. "I plan

to make myself available to Quinn for when he tires of you."
She eyed Sarah up and down. "Which won't be long, I'm
sure."

Sarah clenched her fists under her apron skirt. It was true.
There was nothing special about her appearance. She'd even
overheard one of her uncle's gang say she looked two days
of hard riding from pretty—at least she thought they were
talking about her. Why would Quinn want her when he
could have a beauty like Florinda—even if the woman was as
prickly as a cactus?

Miss Phillips lifted her chin, spun back into her room, and
slammed the door. Sarah stood there stunned. Never in her
life had anyone directed such a vicious verbal attack toward
her and made her feel so insignificant. She'd always been a
peacemaker, and most folks liked her because of her kind ways.

Worry swirled in her mind like a dirt devil, spinning and
gyrating up negative thoughts.

Did Quinn regret being forced to marry her?

Would he send her and the children packing even before his
grandmother died? Which didn't look to be anytime soon. Or
was she doomed to live her days in a marriage with a husband
who didn't love her?

She rushed to her room, tears streaming down her cheeks.
At the settee, she fell to her knees and laid her arms on the
cushion and cried. After a few minutes, she lifted her head
and dried her eyes.

Nothing would be accomplished by giving in to her worries.
There was only one thing that would help. She lifted her face
toward the ceiling. *Please, Father, show me how to make my
husband love me and not Florinda. Teach me how to be gracious
even to her.*

❧

"Good afternoon, Quinn."

The sound of Florinda's voice so near made Quinn cringe.

He continued uncinching his horse and tossed the saddle over one shoulder. Maybe the odor of sweaty horse would drive the woman back to the house. She was more persistent than a swarm of gnats.

He nodded to her as he passed by, walked into the barn, and slung his saddle and pad over a block in the tack room. He grabbed a grooming brush and turned to exit the stuffy area, but Florinda blocked the doorway. Why was she sticking closer to him than a sand burr?

Maybe if he quit avoiding her he would find out. "Did you need something?"

Florinda's pink lips wrinkled in a pout he was sure some men found charming. But he wasn't one of them. "You've been so busy since I arrived that we haven't had time to talk."

"A ranch is a busy place."

She spun the handle of a lacy pink parasol that rested against one shoulder. "I've missed chatting with you. It's been two years since I last saw you."

So? he wanted to say. And when did they ever chat with each other? She gabbed, while he tried to talk with the men or get away from her. He'd never seen her do an ounce of work. Never once offered to help his mother the previous times she'd visited. As far as he was concerned, she was as useful as one of those odd French poodle dogs that one of his grandmother's wealthy friends in Bismarck owned.

He resisted heaving a sigh. Some host he was. "What did you want to talk about?"

Her lips twisted in a wry grin. "Tell me how you met Sarah."

"Why?" He narrowed his eyes. What did that matter? Florinda already looked down on his wife. She didn't need more ammunition.

"Oh, just curious. She doesn't seem the kind of woman you'd choose to marry."

Sweat trickled down his temple from the closed-in room. He didn't normally stay in the small, windowless area any longer than was necessary. Besides not having ventilation, it reminded him of when he'd been locked up in Will's jail for a crime he hadn't committed. He moved closer to the door, but Florinda didn't back up. She gazed up at him as if he was her long lost love. He swallowed the lump that rose to his throat.

He wanted to shove his way past her, to completely ignore her, but her father had bought a lot of cattle from him over the years. He couldn't afford to lose Tom's business because of a row with his daughter. At least near the door he could breathe in fresher air. "Just tell me what you want, Florinda. I have work to do."

She cocked her head and batted her lashes. "I want to go riding with you. To see your ranch."

He didn't have time for casual riding, but if it meant keeping Tom's business, he'd have to make time for it, unless he could discourage her. "You know we don't have any sidesaddles."

For a moment the young woman's composure seemed rattled. "Couldn't you borrow one from someone?"

He shook his head. The nearest neighbor was nearly an hour's ride from him, and none of them owned sidesaddles. "If you want to ride, you'll have to do it astride."

Florinda's lips pursed. "All right, I'll manage. If it means spending time alone with you."

❧

Florinda alternated between pouting and struggling to stay on her horse as the caravan traversed the rocky countryside. John and Tom drove the supply wagon, and Tom cast concerned glances at his daughter every few minutes. Sarah held back a smile, not wanting to take too much pleasure in the other woman's discomfort, but she had brought it upon herself by trying to get Quinn to ride alone with her. Sarah swatted at a mosquito on her hand and then adjusted her felt hat.

She rocked along, comfortable on the bay mare Quinn had saddled for her. If they stayed, would he give her a horse of her own? She'd never had one before but had learned to ride on her father's big mule. The little mare was much less intimidating.

Beth waved with one hand while keeping a hold on the saddle horn with the other. Sarah felt sure her sister was safe riding in front of Quinn. He wouldn't let her fall.

Ryan rode alone on her right on a black gelding with a white diamond on his face. Her brother looked happier than she'd seen him in months. He saw her watching and smiled. "This was a good idea Quinn had, wasn't it?"

She nodded, remembering how Quinn had approached her about riding with him and Florinda.

"I'm in a bind," he'd said. "I'm hoping you'll help me out. Florinda asked me to take her riding, but I don't want to go alone, and I've got the ranch hands all working on projects." He stared at the ground a moment and then looked up with those coffee brown eyes. "Would you go riding with us?"

That he didn't want to be alone with Miss Phillips set Sarah's delight soaring. Other than to care for his grandmother, it was the first thing he'd ever asked of her. "What if we took the children, too?"

Quinn nodded and smiled, stirring her heart. He smiled so rarely that when he did it was a magnificent sight. "Good idea."

When they'd told the children at dinner about the ride the next day, the men had begged to come along. Ryan mentioned an overnight ride, and the next thing she knew, a camping trip to sleep under the stars had been planned. Florinda was the only one scowling at the table. Sarah sighed. She'd hoped the prissy city gal would decide not to go, but that wasn't the case. At least Florinda wasn't out riding the range alone with Quinn.

Camp was set up alongside a tributary of the Little Missouri River. Cottonwood trees sheltered them from the warm summer sun, and an abundance of knee-high grass kept the stock well-fed. Quinn had gone hunting for some meat for dinner while Tom and Uncle John attempted to start a fire. Sarah grinned at their feeble effort. If they didn't improve, everyone would be eating cold biscuits and cheese for dinner.

Two rough tents had been erected for the women from quilts strung over rope that had been tied to tree branches. Sarah laid out additional quilts and wool blankets for her and Beth to sleep on and then put several in Florinda's tent also. With that chore done, she turned to check on the children. Both of them had headed down to the creek as soon as the supplies had been unloaded from the pack horse. She could just barely see the top of Ryan's head.

Florinda sat on a log, looking completely out of place in her frilly blouse and the brown split riding skirt Quinn had insisted she wear. Her fancy hat was tied down with wide lavender netting and secured in a showy bow under her chin. She flicked a leaf off her lap.

Ryan approached Miss Phillips, holding something behind his back. Beth followed her brother, giggling with her hand over her mouth. Sarah's stomach tightened. What were those two up to?

Her brother stuck out his hand and dropped something into Florinda's lap. She looked down, and her bored features transformed into horror. She soared to her feet, dancing and screeching so loud that the horses tethered to a nearby line backed up and snorted. Laughing, Ryan and Beth disappeared in the nearby bushes. Uncle John jumped up and jogged toward the horses.

Tom Phillips spun around and raced toward his daughter. "What's wrong?"

"Oh! Th–those horrible children."

Tom's gaze surveyed his daughter from head to toe. "Are you hurt?"

Florinda dusted her skirt with jerky hands and scanned the ground. Sarah knew the moment she spotted the frog.

"There! They put that horrid creature on my lap. Oh, Father, I'll probably get warts now." She fell into Tom's arms and he loosely patted her. His questioning gaze collided with Sarah's, and she pointed to the frog. Tom's mouth swerved to one side. He stepped back, looking embarrassed and annoyed. "It's just a toad. It can't hurt you."

Sarah grabbed the innocent frog and couldn't resist holding it up. "I'll just take him back to the creek. I'm sorry it frightened you."

Florinda shrank back. "Those rotten children should be punished for scaring me half to death."

Tom patted her shoulder. "Now, now, they were just having some fun."

Puffing up, Florinda glared at Sarah. "Their behinds should be paddled good and hard."

Sarah narrowed her eyes and walked past Uncle John, doubting Florinda had ever had a spanking. He pounded two rocks together in an attempt to spark some kindling to life. "Elke put some matches in the crate with the cooking pots."

John straightened and gave her a perplexed but humorous stare. "We have matches? You knew that and let us make a fool of ourselves for the last half hour?"

Sarah grinned. "I didn't want to spoil your fun."

He chuckled and shook his head then walked toward the crates of supplies. Sarah set the frog on the creek bank and took in the tranquil setting. Water bubbled along the rocky bed, gurgling its way to the mouth of the Little Missouri. She probably should punish the children. But they were just playing and having fun. She rubbed her neck. What would her mother have done?

Tears blurred her eyes as she remembered her parents. She'd never wanted to be fully responsible for the children and didn't know how to handle a situation like this one. If only her mother could give her advice—could hug her one more time. She'd never even had a chance to say good-bye.

Beth giggled off to her right, and Sarah turned to see her siblings squatting in the dirt near the creek bank. What were they up to now?

"Look at this huge one." Beth dangled a squirming worm in the air.

"Yep, that fellow's big and fat." Ryan took the worm and placed it in an empty can.

Sarah tiptoed nearer. "Just what are you two doing?"

Beth jumped and studied the ground, as if afraid to look Sarah in the eye. Ryan shrugged one shoulder. "Just digging up worms. Quinn said he'd take us fishing."

Sarah eyed the two, not sure if she believed them. Beth looked too suspicious. "You are not going to put those in Miss Phillips's lap."

Ryan glanced up, shaking his head. "Of course not. Her screaming just about broke my hearing."

"Mine, too." Beth rubbed her ears.

Sarah shoved her hands to her waist. "She wouldn't have been screaming if you hadn't dropped a frog in her lap."

Beth's eyes glistened with tears. "I told him not to do that."

Ryan's head jerked toward his sister. "You did not. You were just afraid to touch the frog and made me do it."

Sarah sighed and stooped down. "It doesn't matter whose idea it was. You will both go apologize right now or you won't have dinner."

Ryan scowled and Beth nodded. Sarah glanced up at the sky. *Oh, Lord, give me patience and wisdom.*

❧

The fragrant scent of cooked prairie chickens filled the air, making Quinn's stomach growl. The traps he and Ryan had set earlier had captured five birds. Sarah and Beth scurried around getting the food items Elke had sent with them ready. Nobody would go hungry tonight.

Ryan held up a plump burlap sack stuffed with grouse feathers that he'd picked up off the ground. "That's all of them."

"Good job. Grandma will be happy to have more feathers for stuffing pillows. Put the sack in the wagon and wash up. Dinner's about ready."

The boy nodded and cast him a shy grin. "That plucking contest was fun."

Quinn ruffled Ryan's hair. "It was indeed. You almost beat your sisters."

Ryan's face puckered. "I would have if you hadn't let Beth help Sarah."

"I don't think she was as much help as you believe she was." Quinn chuckled, as he remembered watching Tom and Uncle John yanking feathers as fast as they could. When they returned home, he could imagine the stories they'd be telling their friends and associates. Florinda had turned up her nose and strode off to read a book when asked if she wanted to participate. She didn't have one-fourth the gumption that Sarah did.

Ryan walked toward the wagon, the sack of feathers over one shoulder. The boy was certainly thawing. Quinn was grateful for that. He still regretted his outburst when he first saw the children that day he and Sarah were married. He wasn't one to lose control. The campfire flickered and popped as he stared into it.

"Dinner's ready." Sarah held out a plate to him.

Quinn grasped it, and for a moment, Sarah didn't release the other side. It was as if they were connected. His gaze captured hers, and he felt as if sizzling lightning connected them. Why did she move him like no other woman had? She wasn't gorgeous in the face like Florinda, but she had an inner beauty and kindness that Miss Phillips would never have. Did Sarah feel anything for him?

He blinked, surprised at the train of thought that rippled through him. He pulled the plate from Sarah's hand and stepped back as if he'd been burned. When had he started caring for her?

Questions filled Sarah's gaze, but she turned away.

"I fixed a biscuit for you." Beth handed a plate to Florinda, who eyed it with unhidden speculation.

"I—uh—thank you." Miss Phillips lifted the roasted thigh and leg of the prairie chicken and peered under it, then set it down. She stirred her spoon cautiously through the cabbage slaw that Elke had sent, examining it, and then picked up the biscuit and studied it for a moment.

Beth hurried back to Ryan, snickering. The boy's eyes flickered with delight, and both kids spun toward Florinda. Quinn's gut tightened.

She lifted the top half of the biscuit off and stared. Quinn was ten feet away, but he was certain he saw something move. The young woman's eyes went wide and her mouth opened, but no sound came out. She leapt to her feet, dropping the tin plate to the ground, and shrieked. Everyone in camp jumped, except Quinn and the kids. Beth covered her ears and grinned. Ryan rolled in the dirt near the campfire, laughing, as Sarah spun around. Three fat worms wriggled off the biscuit and onto the ground.

Tom hurried toward his daughter, but she pivoted and marched red-faced toward Quinn. "You will take me back to the ranch this instant. I will not stay here and allow those hooligans to frighten another ten years off me. This is no place for a lady."

thirteen

With a lantern spilling light over the creek bank, Sarah washed the last of the dinner dishes. She rinsed them in the creek and dumped out the sudsy water. She gave each plate and fork a final rinse then put them in the bucket to dry.

Tom had offered to return home with his daughter, but Quinn insisted that he take her since Tom wasn't familiar with the ranch and might get lost in the dark. Sarah was pretty sure Tom was relieved. Both he and John were enjoying themselves immensely. Camping was so far removed from their normal routine of office work and dealing with beef buyers. She understood their reluctance to leave a place with no responsibilities or pressures.

Somehow, Sarah felt Florinda had gotten just what she wanted—a ride alone with Quinn. And in the dark, no less. She shouldn't be jealous, but when Florinda had claimed her fear was too great to ride alone, Quinn had allowed her to sit in front of him. Sarah couldn't stand the thought of her husband's arms around that woman. Florinda was probably leaning back against Quinn's chest, enjoying every minute and gloating in the dark.

She should have gone with him. But the children had been so excited about sleeping under the stars. They'd whined and complained about it when they'd lived with Uncle Harlan, but on the Rocking M, it was a great adventure. Still, she'd sent her siblings to bed without dessert, much to their complaint. They deserved a harsher punishment for disobeying her and for scaring Miss Phillips again, but she couldn't bring herself to spank them.

Sarah shook her head remembering how Ryan adamantly argued that she hadn't told them not to scare Miss Phillips but rather not to put any more critters *on* her.

She picked up the bucket and lantern and made her way back to camp. Uncle John and Tom had already bedded down. Ryan wiggled around on his pallet as if he couldn't get comfortable. Sarah peeked at Beth and found her little sister was sound asleep.

She set the lantern on the wagon's tailgate and put the bucket behind it. Out in the darkness a horse nickered. Sarah jumped. As always her first thoughts raced to Uncle Harlan. Had he figured out that she took the gold to Medora? Was the story still circulating of the rancher who married a jailbird? What if he had heard about it and was on his way to the Rocking M right now?

All security fled, and she yanked a rifle from the buckboard. She stepped into the shadows and aimed toward where she'd heard the horse.

"H'lo the camp."

Ryan and John sat up in unison and looked around. Tom and Beth slept on.

"Who's there?" Sarah called, clutching the rifle with trembling hands.

"It's Slim. Quinn sent me up here to help y'all with breakfast tomorrow and to get packed up and back to the house." Bushes rattled as he passed between them and into the light, leading his horse. One of the tethered horses nickered to Slim's horse. The cowboy tipped his hat. "Evening, ma'am."

Sarah exhaled a relieved breath. "C'mon in. There's coffee left."

She poured him a cup while he unsaddled his horse and spread out his bedroll a few yards from the campfire. She handed him the tin cup, then crawled into the tent. Sarah rebraided her hair as she stared at the flickering flames of the campfire. Why had Quinn sent Slim instead of coming back himself?

Probably because Miss Phillips wouldn't release her hold on him. No doubt the persnickety woman had wrangled some other chore for Quinn to do. Now that she had him to herself, Sarah was certain Florinda would make the most of it.

She lay down but doubted she would sleep much. Too many worries swirled in her mind. Quinn had wanted their marriage to be one only on paper. Could Florinda steal Quinn's love?

Sarah flipped onto her other side as she realized how ridiculous that thought was. If Quinn had affections for Miss Phillips, he never would have married another woman. Still. . . Florinda was beautiful to look at, and Sarah was just as she'd said—a tumbleweed.

She flopped onto her back and stared up at the stars through the open end of the tent. There were millions of them sprinkling the raven sky like little diamonds she'd once seen in a store. Quinn might not love her, but he was an honorable man. He wouldn't share his affections with a woman when he was married to another.

God had put her and Quinn together. Sarah was certain of it. The Lord had answered her prayers in a manner she never could have imagined and provided a home for her and the children. He wouldn't let them be cast out because of a spoiled, selfish woman.

"Thank You, Father, for calming my fears. Forgive me for worrying overly much and not trusting You to take care of us. I ask You to forgive me for being jealous of Florinda, and help me to be nicer to her. Thank You for keeping Uncle Harlan away, and please don't let him find us." She shivered at the thought of what he might do if he did.

An unwanted tear ran down the corner of her eye. "Please

show me how to love Quinn, and make him learn to care for me, so we can stay here forever."

❧

The closer they rode to home, the more anxious Sarah became. It was stupid. She knew that, but her fears threatened to overpower the peacefulness she'd felt that morning as she prayed by the creek.

"Are you cold, Sissy?"

"No, I'm fine. Why?" Though late June and normally a one-blanket night, sleeping outside had felt much cooler than in her cozy bedroom. She wished she'd thought to bring a shawl along.

"You're shivering." Beth squeezed her arms around Sarah's waist. "I'll keep you warm."

She patted her sister's hand. The ranch yard was quiet as they rode into it. Ryan trotted his horse over to the corral and climbed down, but Sarah aimed hers for the house. The front door opened, and Quinn strode out with Florinda on his arm. Her heart dropped, and her whole body felt weak, as if she'd lived through a train wreck. Had she lost him already?

Quinn smiled at her, and unwound Florinda's arm so quickly that the prissy woman dressed in pale green nearly stumbled. She grabbed hold of the porch post and scowled. Quinn didn't notice as he bounded down the steps toward Sarah. His warm smile set Sarah's hope back on track.

"Let me help you down, Beth." The little girl nearly leapt from her seat behind Sarah and hugged Quinn's neck.

"I didn't like it when you left."

"Neither did I, sweet thing. Elke has some cinnamon rolls on the warmer. Why don't you wash up and go get one."

Beth grinned at him and kicked her feet. Quinn set her down, and she took off like a top. His gaze turned upward, and a shy smile tugged at one corner of his mouth.

"I missed you." He lifted his hands, stunning Sarah.

He missed her? Ignoring Florinda's glare, she fell into his arms and wrapped herself around her husband. Was he serious? Or was it all a show to get Miss Phillips to leave him alone?

Quinn gently pushed her away from his warm chest and stared down. He brushed a strand of hair from her face and tucked it behind her ear, making her knees go weak. She loved his dark, expressive eyes and longed to run her hand through his hair. He leaned down, pushed her hat back on her head, and claimed her lips. Sarah was so surprised that she stood there stiff as a step for a moment until her senses returned. Then she kissed him back, showing him that she longed to be his true wife. Quinn inhaled sharply through his nose, as if her response surprised him.

He set her back far too soon and stared into her eyes. Sarah's heart ricocheted in her chest. She was afraid she was falling in love with a man who didn't want her. But his kiss had felt anything but phony.

He smiled, and it actually reached his eyes. "I'm sorry Florinda ruined our campout, and I hope you realize that there's nothing between her and me. If I've given you that impression, I'm sorry. You're my wife, Sarah, and that's what's important."

Quinn smiled openly as he tucked her under one arm and held her close. "Ryan, come and tend your sister's horse."

The boy jogged toward them, casting curious glances as he grabbed the horse's reins.

"Be sure to brush her down and feed her."

"Yes, sir." He nodded and led the mare toward the barn.

Sarah grinned, pleased to see her brother responding so well to Quinn's orders. When he first arrived, he hardly wanted anything to do with the man, but now he shadowed Quinn whenever he could—almost like a father and son.

With her arm around her husband's narrow waist, Sarah

allowed Quinn to guide her up the steps. She nodded at Florinda, whose lips looked as if they'd tasted lemonade without the sugar. She crossed her arms, stomped one foot, and sashayed back inside. Sarah wished that she and Florinda could be friends in spite of their mutual attraction to Quinn, but it was obvious that Miss Phillips didn't share that desire.

The cabin smelled of cinnamon and fresh baked bread. Even though they'd eaten breakfast at the camp, now that her worries had been calmed, Sarah's stomach begged for food.

Florinda must have gone to her bedroom, for she was nowhere in sight. In spite of the woman's immature display, Sarah couldn't help grinning up at Quinn. Gloating was wrong, she knew that, but her heart overflowed with so much happiness at her husband's surprising greeting that she couldn't hold it all in.

Martha hurried toward them, dressed in a brown and gold calico. "Welcome back, dear. I missed your company and those ornery children. Beth's in the kitchen, having a snack. Perhaps you'd like to join her when you're finished with my grandson?"

She looked up at Quinn, enjoying his nearness and the feel of his solid body. He smiled. "I'm glad you're back, but work is waiting. I'll see you at lunch." He cast a quick glance at his grandmother, bent down and kissed Sarah's cheek, and then all but bolted for the barn.

Martha tugged Sarah's arm around her own and patted her hand. Her eyes twinkled. "Well, things are certainly looking up between you and my grandson. It's amazing what a little competition can do."

ða

After breakfast the next morning, Sarah sat on the sofa in the parlor, helping Beth with her alphabet. She wrote an *M* on the slate. "What's that letter?"

Beth grinned up at her. "That one's easy. It's an *M*, like the Rocking M on Quinn's sign."

"That's right. How about this one?" She wiped off the letter and replaced it with a *Q*.

A rustling sounded from the hall, and Sarah looked over her shoulder. Florinda strode into the room with her fancy hat affixed to her head and tied under her chin with a big bow. She set a satchel on a chair, laid her parasol beside it, and narrowed her eyes at Sarah. "I'm leaving. Have someone get a buggy and drive me into town."

Sarah set Beth on the floor. "Go to the barn and find Quinn, please." The girl bounded out the door, casting an odd look back at Miss Phillips.

Sarah set the slate and chalk on the sofa and stood. What could she say to make Florinda reconsider? Would her leaving affect her father's decision to buy cattle from Quinn? The men had been talking numbers and prices yesterday evening, but nothing had been settled, as far as she knew.

"Please, won't you sit down and talk about this? There's no need for you to leave." Sarah locked her fingers together to keep her hands from shaking. "I was hoping we might become friends."

Florinda lifted her nose and tossed her head. "That's not possible."

"But why? What have I done to make you dislike me so?"

"Surely you realize that I have had my eye on Quinn for many years."

"How could I know?" Sarah shook her head. "Honestly. I knew nothing about you when Quinn and I married. I'll admit that I don't understand your interest in him, when it's obvious that you don't like it here."

Miss Phillips turned up her nose. "I can barely stand to visit this rustic place, but I had plans for Quinn in my father's beef production company."

"He would never be happy in a city. He's a rancher at heart and needs the wide open spaces, and this ranch needs him."

"Well. . .it's neither here nor there now. I probably should have set my sights for Adam. At least he had the sense to leave this godforsaken place."

Loud footsteps sounded a moment before Quinn, John, and Tom entered the parlor. Mr. Phillips strode to his daughter's side. "What's this I hear about you leaving?"

"It's true. I can't stay here another day."

Tom scratched his head. "Well. . .you can't travel alone." He turned to face the other men. "I'm sorry, but it looks like I'll be leaving today. My daughter can't travel unescorted. Go ahead with the numbers we talked about. I'll send my man out here in mid-September, unless I hear different from you. All right?"

Quinn nodded and held out his hand. "Thank you. I'll make sure you get quality beef."

Florinda squirmed and fiddled with her net bow. John stared at his friend, looking disappointed and perplexed.

Tom pursed his lips and stared at the floor; then he looked at John. "I'm sorry our trip was cut short, but—"

John laid his hand on his friend's shoulder. "Think nothing more of it. Family comes first. I'll see you when I get back to Chicago."

Tom nodded and walked to Martha, who'd just entered the room. "I'm sorry to be leaving so soon, but I thank you for your wonderful hospitality." Tom hurried down the hall to his room.

"I'll get a buggy ready and take you to town." Quinn tipped his hat at Florinda.

"I'd prefer someone else drive us."

Sarah's heart ached for Quinn at Florinda's rude tone. Now that Miss Phillips had conceded her loss, she no longer wanted to be around him.

"No problem." Quinn pressed his lips tight and glanced at Sarah. She tried to soften things with a smile. "I'll have one of the hands drive you to town."

Quinn spun around and stalked out of the room in wide, long-legged strides.

Now that Florinda was leaving, would he continue showing affection to Sarah? She was asleep when he finally went to bed last night and had only seen him at breakfast. He'd smiled at her but hadn't touched her since greeting her in the yard.

Sarah collected the slate and chalk and put it in a desk drawer. Florinda paced in front of the window, waiting for her father. Sarah couldn't help feeling sorry for the man who had to cut his plans short because of his daughter's whims. Maybe if Florinda's mother were still alive things would be different.

"Can I offer you some refreshment before you leave?"

The young woman spun around. "No, you may not. And I would appreciate if you would leave my sight immediately."

Sarah cringed at Florinda's command but didn't want to upset their guest further. "As you wish. I will pray that you have a safe journey home." She hurried into the kitchen and ran straight into Martha's arms.

"Now don't fret, dear. That girl never liked coming here." The older woman patted her back and leaned close to Sarah's ear. "I'm tired of her childish games."

"I'm sorry. I never meant to cause problems for you and Quinn."

Martha pushed away. "You didn't, and I won't have you thinking that. Quinn's been the happiest I've seen since Anna's wedding. You're good for my grandson, and you need to know that."

Sarah forced a smile, grateful for Martha's encouragement. "Thank you."

Martha patted her cheek. "Just give Quinn more time. I can already tell that he has feelings for you. He just needs to realize it himself."

fourteen

Quinn sat at his desk, calculating how much he'd make from the sale of one hundred twenty head of cattle to Tom Phillips. The amount would more than see them through the next winter and leave plenty of stock so that he'd have a good crop of calves next spring, as long as the winter wasn't too harsh.

Balancing everything wasn't always easy, but it was doable. He laid down his pen and leaned back in the chair. Thank goodness Tom had more sense than his spoiled daughter.

Lamplight flickered across his ledger pages. In spite of having more people at the ranch to provide for, things were going well. He thought of the two pair of Percherons in training. In another few weeks he would be receiving final payment for the four large stock horses.

Yep, things were going well, but he still had a dissatisfaction that he couldn't shake. Was it because of Sarah?

His mouth curved up as he thought of how surprised she'd been when he'd kissed her the morning after the campout. And she had pleasantly amazed him by kissing him back quite soundly. Her mouth was as soft as a horse's muzzle, and she felt good in his arms. He'd been a fool to want a marriage in name only, but then, he hadn't really wanted a marriage at all. Yeah, he'd willingly married Sarah, because it had seemed the right thing to do at the time. He got a wife and got Grandma off his back and got Sarah out of jail. What would have happened to Ryan and Beth if he hadn't married Sarah?

Quinn ran his hand through his hair, not wanting to think of how bad things could have been for the children. Maybe

Sarah would be willing to consider a true marriage. She certainly hadn't liked how Florinda threw herself at him.

"What are you grinning at?" Sarah's soft voice floated out of the surrounding darkness a moment before he saw her.

He straightened, knowing he couldn't tell her his thoughts. Or could he?

Sarah shrugged. "Never mind. I just wanted to ask you something."

"Shoot."

"Well. . .I've been having evening devotions with Ryan and Beth ever since our parents died. Pa used to lead them, and I've tried to keep that one thing going when everything else was going haywire."

Quinn stood and crossed the room to her. "That's good that you have. I'm sure it's helped the kids."

"It helped me, too. It would have been so easy to get angry at God for all that happened." She glanced up at him, her blue eyes swimming with tears. "But then, who would I have had to help me? I would have been completely alone if not for God."

He placed his hands on Sarah's upper arms. "You have us now. You're not alone anymore." Sarah's smile warmed a place in his heart that had been cold for a long time.

"I don't want you to be alone either." She placed her hand on his chest. "Don't think I haven't noticed how you try to keep yourself apart from everyone else. You don't have to bear your burdens alone, Quinn. I'm here to help, and God will help."

He knew she was right. At one time, he was close to his heavenly Father, but the pressures of life and the busyness of the ranch had pressed in, and before he knew it, he'd quit praying and seeking God.

"Martha mentioned she'd like to hold family devotions before the children went to bed." Sarah nibbled the corner of her lower lip and glanced up at him through her lashes. "We were wondering if you'd be willing to lead them."

Quinn stiffened and walked back to his desk, putting space between him and Sarah. Who was he to be leading folks in devotions? Yeah, maybe he stood up in front of the ranch hands on Sundays when they couldn't go into town, but teaching children. . .what if he said the wrong thing? And how could a man who'd been walking between believing in God and chucking all he'd learned out the window lead others in their walk with the good Lord?

"I don't think that would be a good idea."

"What's not?" Sarah's brow puckered. "Having devotions or you leading them?"

He remained silent, not wanting to admit that he was a failure in the spiritual realm. He'd turned his back on God when things had gotten tough, and it didn't seem right to go crawling back now that times were better.

Sarah strolled toward him. "You don't have to make up your mind now. Just think about it. Please. Ryan could use a man's example in this area, too. You've been such an encouragement to him." Sarah laid her hand on Quinn's arm. "Ryan has opened up and isn't so angry since you've been showing him how to do ranch work. Thank you for that."

She stood on her tiptoes and leaned toward him. Quinn's heart raced double-time having her so near. He leaned down, and she placed a warm kiss on his cheek. "Good night, Quinn."

Her gentle smile stayed with him long after she'd gone to bed. He paced the length of the parlor and back several times, finally stopping in front of the window. The glow of the lantern reflected back at him, as he stared into the inky darkness outside.

Closing his eyes, he thought of Sarah's words. *"You don't have to bear your burdens alone, Quinn. I'm here to help, and God will help."*

Sarah had made things easier for his grandmother and had

taken over much of caring for the house. She'd freed him from worrying about Grandma so he could concentrate more on the ranch, and she'd reminded him that God was there to help, too. Perhaps it was time he reacquainted himself with his heavenly Father. Time he quit running from God.

He knelt in front of a chair and bent his head. "Lord, I don't deserve to ask for Your mercy. I've been stubbornly operating on my own since my pa died, but I need Your help. I miss Your closeness. Forgive me, Father God."

❧

Sarah ran the needle through the two pieces of fabric. She loved sitting on the porch and sewing. All too soon winter would wrap them in its cold fist, and they wouldn't be able to enjoy the outdoors like they could now. She checked on her sister and smiled. Beth sat at the far end of the porch, playing with a litter of kittens.

"I don't like to say it, but I'm glad to have Florinda gone. My stomach was all a-swirl when she was flitting around." Martha selected a triangle of fabric and compared it to the one she'd just stitched. She shook her head, picked another one, and started sewing. "I don't know why she comes here. She's always bored, even when she visited my home in Bismarck."

"I feel badly for the shameless way I acted when she was here. I should have been kinder to her." Sarah's hands dropped to her lap. Some Christian she was. Her first chance to act as hostess and all she could do was to fight like crazy to keep her husband from noticing a prettier, more sophisticated woman.

Martha smiled. "I rather enjoyed watching you fight for my grandson's attention—and if I'm not mistaken, I believe he enjoyed it, too."

Heat rushed to Sarah's cheeks. She closed her eyes and laid her head against the rocker. "Was I that obvious? I'm mortified."

"Don't be." Martha squeezed Sarah's hand. "It warms my heart to see Quinn so happy."

"You think he's happy?" Sarah looked at Martha. Her gray hair was neatly packed into a bun pinned at her nape. Wisps of white danced around her face, and soft brown eyes held hers.

"Oh, yes. I guess you could say he's thawed since you and the children came here. For so long, he focused only on the ranch. It hurt his relationship with Anna and Adam and even with his mother. I think that's why Ellen stayed in Bismarck after I broke my leg. She and Quinn were quite close, but then he seemed to pull away. Maybe he didn't feel as needed with the twins finding mates and getting married. I'm so thankful he has you now."

Sarah considered whether to tell Martha the truth about her relationship with Quinn. But how could she steal Martha's joy? No, she and Quinn would have to work it out on their own.

Resuming her stitching, she thought about the previous evening when she'd talked with Quinn. She'd gone in there fully planning to tell him about her uncle and the danger she might have brought to the Rocking M, but instead she'd asked him about devotions. How could her plans go so haywire?

Tonight. She'd find a way to warn him tonight. They'd been at the Rocking M close to a month now, and surely Uncle Harlan had returned home and discovered his gold gone. He wouldn't know which way they'd gone, but most likely he'd assume it was Medora since it was the closest town. Maybe by the time he got there talk would have died down.

She could only hope. *Please, Father, don't let him find us. And keep everyone at the Rocking M safe.*

Ryan rode up to the front porch and pushed his hat back on his face. The sun had lightened his hair and darkened his skin, adding to the patch of freckles on his nose and cheeks.

He looked so happy and at ease in the saddle. "So, are we going riding like you promised?"

Beth set down a plain white kitten with a tabby tail and ran over to join them. "Yeah, you said you'd take us riding after lunch if Quinn couldn't."

"I was hoping to complete the main squares today." Sarah ran her hand over the colorful quilt pieces in her lap, but it could wait until this evening. Keeping her promise to the kids was more important.

"You go ahead. I can finish this." Martha gently removed the sewing from Sarah's hands.

"Looks like we're going riding." She grinned at her siblings.

"Yippee!" Beth clapped her hands together. "Do I getta ride my own horse?"

"No, you'd better ride with me until Quinn has time to help you more." Sarah stood and stretched, ignoring Beth's pout. She ducked inside and took Anna's old hat from the peg it rested on. Life at the Rocking M was busy, but not like it had been at Uncle Harlan's place. She'd worked from dawn to dusk, hunting, skinning, or plucking their food and trying to keep the kids away from the outlaw gang.

Ryan lifted Beth onto his horse, and they rode toward the barn. Sarah followed, but a shiver sent goose bumps across her arms. Eddie, the youngest of the outlaw gang, had constantly leered at her and tried to catch her alone. She might have been a chicken and always kept the children close, but his pale blue gaze unnerved her—and not in a good way. Not like Quinn's steady gaze did.

But Eddie was gone, and she was a married woman for now. She twisted the gold band that Martha had given Quinn to give to her. Somehow wearing it made her feel more married.

Ryan quickly saddled the bay mare, and with Beth in front of her in the saddle, Sarah followed her brother up a hill.

They rode for a good half hour. Tendrils from Beth's blond hair tickled her face. The sun threatened to toast them, but the ever-present breeze cooled her body. She'd miss these days when the weather turned frigid and snow covered everything, just like flour did whenever Beth helped with the baking.

They rode for nearly an hour when Beth looked over her shoulder, her blue eyes pleading. "I'm hot. Can we go splash in the creek?"

It was often hard to say no to the little imp, but today she didn't have to. "I think that's a grand idea. You want to join us, Ryan?"

The boy scowled. Ever since Quinn had taught him to ride, he hadn't wanted to get off a horse. Why, he'd probably sleep in the barn if she'd let him. At least he was happy. After a moment his expression softened. "Sure. Why not."

At the creek, they watered the horses, and then Sarah led them to a patch of grass to graze while the kids prepared to play in the water. Beth quickly shed her shoes and socks and tiptoed into the gurgling stream. At its deepest point, the narrow creek didn't even reach Beth's knees.

Ryan ran back to join them, a wide smile on his face. His boots flew in different directions and his socks quickly followed. He rolled up his pants, revealing legs as pale as the ivory fabric in her quilt. He hopped in, heedless of the rocks on the bank and in the water.

Sarah smiled, so delighted that he was a carefree boy again. Quinn had helped make that happen, and she owed him. Beth giggled and cupped a handful of water and tossed it at her brother. Not to be outdone, he splashed wave after wave at Beth. She squealed and ran the opposite direction.

Cottonwoods created a pleasant canopy overhead, allowing dappled sunlight to filter between the branches. The wind whispered through the leaves. Sarah reclined on a sun-roasted boulder near the water and watched the dancing limbs overhead. When her parents had died and they lost their farm, she thought nothing worse could ever happen, but it had. Being so helplessly locked up in jail and fearing for Ryan and Beth had been worse. But she never could have imagined how landing in jail could have turned out so wonderful. Her mother had often told her that the Bible says "all things work together for good to them that love God, to them who are the called according to his purpose." She'd remained close to God in trying times and had prayed for Him to help her get out of jail and to protect the children, and He'd sent a handsome cowboy to rescue them.

She loved watching Quinn move, long-legged but so smooth. And his eyes—almost so brown you couldn't see the pupils. Then there was that curly dark blond hair that she longed to twist around her finger, and his deep voice, which sent vibrations all through her when he talked. She heaved a sigh.

A strange feeling, not unlike the warmth of a mustard plaster, heated her chest. Her eyes bolted open. She loved her husband! The awe of her discovery stunned her. He'd provided a home and protected her and the kids, and somewhere along the way, her admiration had turned to love. Martha's constant boasting about her grandson's virtues hadn't hurt any. She rubbed her hand over her chest, almost expecting to feel heat.

No, things couldn't be any better—unless Quinn loved her, too. Was that too much to hope for?

Beth squealed, and she splashed through the water with Ryan roaring after her. Sarah was happy to see the kids playing together instead of bickering.

If only Quinn loved her. . .then maybe they'd never have to leave the Rocking M. *Please, Lord, show me how to make my husband fall in love with me.*

A twig snapped behind her just as something stepped between her and the sunlight. Beth screamed, but this wasn't a fun squeal. Sarah opened her eyes and bolted up.

No.

Eddie stood beside her, a sickening grin pasted on his whiskery face. Uncle Harlan held Beth, who squirmed and kicked, while Jim wrestled with Ryan. He smacked her brother across the face, and Sarah jumped to her feet. "Don't you hurt him."

Eddie grabbed her arm. "We ain't gonna hurt nobody unless you don't cooperate. Then"—his gaze traveled down her chest—"well, we'll just see."

Sarah's whole body trembled, and her mind raced. How could they get free without one of them getting hurt? *Lord, help us.*

fifteen

Quinn walked out of the barn and headed for the house, ready for supper. Tantalizing fragrances had been emanating from the house for the past hour. Even the enticing odors of beef stew and corn bread that Claude was cooking for the ranch hands had pestered him. Tomorrow he'd tell Sarah to pack him a bigger lunch. He worked hard and had a man-size appetite.

A cloud of dust coming from the direction of the creek snagged his attention. The black horse ran at full gallop. As it neared, Quinn pursed his lips. He'd told Ryan not to run a horse into the ranch yard—and he had Beth with him. Quinn couldn't let this slide. The boy should know better than to endanger his little sister just for some fun.

Quinn lifted his arms to keep the gelding from racing into the barn. Ryan had sense to pull back and slow the animal. Beth nearly fell off as the horse all but slid to a halt. Quinn reached for her and realized she was crying. She clutched his neck and buried her face in his shoulder. He clenched his jaw and glared at Ryan.

His heart skipped. Ryan was crying, too? "What happened?"

The boy tossed his leg over the horse and dropped to the ground. He swiped his sleeve over his eyes and sniffed. "Uncle Harlan and his men have Sarah. They want to swap her for the gold."

Gold, he knew about, but who was this Uncle Harlan? "Beth, go inside and tell Grandma what's happened. Can you do that?"

Beth leaned back and wiped her eyes. "Yes. Will you get

Sissy back?" Her chin and lower lip quivered.

"You bet I will." He hugged the girl and set her down. Her feet were pedaling her toward the door almost the second they hit the ground, keeping pace with his runaway heart. She dashed up the steps and through the door.

Sam and Hank walked out of the barn, covered with sprigs of hay, which they'd been piling in the loft. Quinn nodded with his head for them to join him. "Sarah's been kidnapped."

Both men's eyes widened. With his hands on his hips, Quinn turned back to Ryan. "Tell me everything you know about this Uncle Harlan."

Ryan's face paled, and he studied the ground. "Sarah took us to live with him after our parents died. There were people back in Grand Forks who would have kept us, but we would have been split up. Sarah wouldn't stand for that, so we snuck away one night."

The boy swiped his eyes again and looked up at Quinn. "We didn't know that he was an outlaw."

Quinn straightened, knowing how devastating it must have been for Sarah to learn that when she had hoped that her uncle would care for them. He patted Ryan on the shoulder. "So, what did you do?"

"Things weren't too terrible until three men showed up. Sarah had to hunt every day to find meat for them to eat. She worked awfully hard, but Uncle Harlan always griped at her." Ryan's eyes turned hard. "One man kept pestering her and trying to get her alone."

"You're doing good. Keep going, please."

Ryan shrugged one shoulder. "Sarah wanted to leave, but we didn't have anywhere to go. One day I followed my uncle and discovered where he hid his loot. The next time he and his gang left on a robbing spree, we dug up his money and headed to Medora."

Quinn held up his hand, indicating for Ryan to stop. "Sam,

saddle up my horse and three others. Hank, go find Claude, and both of you get your rifles and any ammunition you've got. I want you two to guard the house."

The men left as ordered, and Quinn nodded for the boy to continue.

"The walk took a lot longer than Sarah thought it would. Then Beth twisted her ankle—" Ryan scowled. "But she was faking just so Sarah would carry her."

"Never mind that. Just finish your story."

He shrugged again. "Sarah left us at the shack where you found us and went to town alone. She said she was going to turn the gold in to the sheriff and get a reward, so we could take the train and get away from Uncle Harlan. We were going to start over."

Quinn crossed his arms and stared off in the distance. Why hadn't Sarah told him she might be in danger? She should have told him. His feelings for her had grown more than he could have believed they ever would. But she hadn't trusted him enough to tell him the truth.

And she hadn't played fair when Florinda had been there. Sarah teased him with her soft caresses, tender looks, and sweet kisses. She shot straight for his heart and scored a bull's-eye. He loved her.

He wanted to slam his fist into a wall, but that would only make him ache more. She should have told him. But he couldn't dwell on that now. "How many men did your uncle have with him? Do you know how much gold he had?"

Ryan straightened and reached over to pet his horse. "Two men, and four hundred and fifty dollars in gold and paper money. I know, I counted it before I told Sarah about it."

Quinn considered the money in a locked box hidden in his bedroom. There wasn't half that much in it. But maybe it was enough to barter for Sarah's life—to distract the outlaws so that he could save her. He closed his eyes. He had to save her.

She'd become important to him. Her soft caresses and stolen kisses had broken down walls that he'd erected years ago. He looked skyward. *Lord, I need Your help here. Show me how to save Sarah. I love her, Lord. I can't lose her.*

He faced Ryan again. "Do you know where the outlaws are now?"

The boy nodded. "Uncle Harlan said they would meet you at that grove of quaking aspens, about a mile west of here. Do you know where it is?" His blue eyes turned hopeful.

"Yep, I do. Take care of your horse and then get inside and stay there."

"But I want to go with you." He grabbed the horse's reins but took a step toward Quinn. "I know how to shoot. I should have protected Sarah."

Quinn pulled him into a hug. "You couldn't fight off three men by yourself. You did what needed to be done. Beth is safe because of you, and I have the information I need to help Sarah. I'm leaving Hank and Claude here to help guard the house. Can you help them?"

Ryan nodded and led his horse to the barn, his back straighter than it had been a few moments ago.

Sam brought his saddled pinto and Quinn's horse out of the barn. Slim and Johnny followed with their own mounts, while Hank and Claude headed for the house. "Make sure your rifles are loaded and be ready to ride in two minutes."

He raced past the two cowpokes, leaving the front door open for them, and ran into his bedroom. First, he located the hidden box and counted out the money he had stored there. Seventy-three dollars was a far cry from what Sarah had stolen from her uncle, but would it be enough to satisfy the man?

He fished around in one of the dresser drawers and found two leather pouches. Maybe he could trick them into thinking he had more money. He filled one with all the paper dollars and gold eagles he had.

Quick footsteps echoed down the hall and stopped at his door. His grandmother stared at him with concerned eyes. "What's this about Sarah gone missing?"

"She's been kidnapped. Do you have some fabric remnants I could have?"

Grandmother blinked and glanced at the pouches. She nodded, disappeared for a moment, and then hurried back into the room with several long strips of calico. "Will this do?"

Quinn nodded. He snatched the cloth and stuffed it in one of the pouches, and tucked a few paper dollars and gold coins into the top of the pouch. He shook the pouch and the coins clinked. That would have to do.

He strapped on the pistols that he rarely wore when working the ranch. His gaze lingered on the settee where Sarah slept each night, and his jaw tightened. He'd bring her back, and they would talk about this fake marriage of theirs.

"Are you going to tell me what's happening?"

Quinn shook his head. "No time. Ask Ryan." He pecked her on the cheek and strode down the hall.

Lord, I know we haven't been on speaking terms as much as we should have, and it's all my fault. But I need Your help. Please, Lord, help me rescue Sarah without her getting hurt.

&

Sarah pressed her hands into her lap. She couldn't quit shaking. Uncle Harlan paced around one tree and then another, stopping to look east every few minutes.

She knew Quinn would come for her, and that scared her to death. What if he got shot because of her? What if the children hadn't made it back home?

She shook her head. No, she couldn't think that. The creek was less than a quarter mile from the house, and you could see the cabin almost the whole way. They made it, and Quinn would be here soon.

She pulled her legs up, making sure her skirts covered her ankles, and laid her head on her knees. *Please, Lord. Help me.*

Uncle Harlan stopped walking and stared eastward again. Then he climbed up on top of a big boulder and looked around. Jim, one of the outlaws, lay next to a smoldering campfire, sound asleep. She could hear his snores from clear across the grove of trees.

She pulled her bound hands to her mouth and tried to bite through the prickly rope. Her wrists ached, and her hands were turning red and going numb. Footsteps snapped a stick and came her way. She looked up, and a chill charged down her spine. Eddie leaned against the nearest aspen; a smirk twisted his lips.

"I told you I'd catch you alone one day." He flicked ashes off the end of his cigarette and watched her uncle as he strode down the path and disappeared around a tall boulder.

Sarah's gaze darted to where she'd last seen her uncle, but he was gone. Her stomach roiled, and her hands trembled.

Eddie tossed down the stub of his cigarette and stomped it out; then he moved toward her like a mountain lion stalking its prey. Sarah pushed away until her back collided with a thirty-foot high butte. The stone felt as cold as Eddie's eyes looked.

Lord, no. Help me.

He grabbed her elbow and pulled her to her feet. She opened her mouth to scream, but his salty fist slapped across it. "Keep quiet, and you won't get hurt. I just want to have some fun. You teased me enough with those looks back at our hideout; now it's time to reward me for my patience."

Sarah kicked and struggled to fight him off, but even with one hand plastered across her mouth, he was too strong. Tears blurred her eyes. Her strength was quickly dwindling.

He shoved her to the ground behind a row of juniper bushes and looked back over his shoulder. With a huge grin on his face, he knelt beside her. Sarah turned into a dust devil, twisting, kicking, and striking out wherever she could.

"Whoa, hold on now."

He shoved back her flailing bound hands and sat down on her belly. A breath gushed out of her, but she kept swinging her arms. "Get off."

Eddie chuckled. "You're a feisty little thing. If I'd known that sooner, I wouldn't have waited so long to press my affections."

He grabbed her hands and forced them over her head. Sarah continued to try to buck him off, but her strength was nearly gone. Eddie leaned down and captured her lips with his.

Sarah squealed and tried to jerk her head away. Suddenly, Eddie froze and fell across her torso. Her breaths came in staccato gulps. Above her, Uncle Harlan's furious gaze caught hers. He held his pistol in his hand, butt facing out.

"I'm sorry, Sarah. I never meant for this to happen. I just want my gold back." He hoisted Eddie off of her and tossed him aside as if he were a sack of potatoes.

"Let's get back to camp."

He pulled her with him, and she barely managed to get her rubbery legs to work. As she passed Eddie, she saw a stain of blood along one side of his head, but she couldn't find it within her to feel sorry for the outlaw. He'd scared her half to death, and if he'd had his way with her, Quinn would never have wanted her.

Sarah shuddered. Her uncle led her back toward the campfire, then suddenly stopped.

"Where's Jim?" He looked around and then stepped backward, scanning the grove of trees and the buttes above.

As far as she could tell, there were no signs that anyone had disturbed their campsite. But where was the other outlaw? Was he laying a trap to snare her uncle so he could get at her?

She had to get a hold of her runaway thoughts. *Help me,*

Lord. Send Quinn to save me, but don't let him get shot.

Her uncle finally shrugged and took her back to where she'd sat before. He pushed down on one of her shoulders. "Just sit there, and this will all be over as soon as I get my money. I'll disappear and forget that my own kin robbed me blind."

He looked more disappointed than angry, but Sarah couldn't work up any sympathy for him. How many people had he killed to get that gold?

Fear and the relief to be free from Eddie made Sarah's limbs weak. She wanted to curl up and sleep and hope that when she woke up, this would all have been a bad dream.

Maybe if she could get her uncle talking, she could get him to set her free. They were kin, after all.

"What happened to you, Uncle Harlan? You're so different than I remember."

He spun around and stared at her. His mouth worked as if he had no teeth and was gumming his meal. He sighed loud and hard and scratched the back of his neck. "After Tildy died, something in me broke. I was never the same. She was my rudder and kept me on the straight and narrow. But when she died, my heart went with her."

"It's never too late to get back on the straight and narrow." Sarah's heart softened toward him. She knew the pain of losing someone you dearly loved. "Pa always hoped you'd come back and help him work the farm. We prayed for you every evening."

"You prayed for me?" He halted his jerky movements and stared at her with wide eyes.

Sarah nodded. The shadows were growing as the sun dipped behind the western hills. It would be dark soon. She had to get away before Eddie came to.

"Well, your prayers didn't do no good."

Something crashed on the other side of the trees as if a

person or animal was coming their way. Harlan spun around and yanked out his pistol. "Who's there?"

Nobody answered, but Sarah couldn't be sure because her heart pounded in her ears.

Uncle Harlan crept in the direction of the noise. "Jim, was that you?"

He kept walking and passed behind a boulder. The second he was out of sight, Sarah pushed to her feet and bolted down the trail toward home. She ran past a line of trees, glanced over her shoulder to see if her uncle was following, and someone grabbed her and threw her to the ground.

She squealed, but another hand slapped across her mouth. She bucked and twisted.

"Stop it, Sarah. It's me."

She froze and looked at Quinn's concerned gaze. He eased up his hand and she gasped for air. He leaned down and kissed her then hauled her up and shoved her behind a boulder.

"Stay there and be quiet. Don't move until I come back."

Quinn crept forward until she could no longer see him. Sarah peered around the big rock.

"We've got your two partners," Quinn said. "You're surrounded, Oakley. Drop your weapon."

Harlan fired in their direction, and the bullet ricocheted off a rock to Sarah's right. She ducked down but couldn't bring herself to quit watching. The campfire behind her uncle made his silhouette a clear target. Quinn fired, hitting the dirt at her uncle's feet. He jumped back, tossed the gun to the ground, and raised his hands. "All right, I give up."

Quinn strode toward him and made quick work of tying him up. "Sam, bring the others out," he yelled and then spun toward her.

Sarah's heart pounded harder with each step he took. She was safe. He'd rescued her again.

She stepped out of the shadows and into her husband's arms. He crushed her against his chest, placing kisses on her head. After a moment, he set her back and stood so that the light of the campfire illuminated him. "Are you all right?"

She nodded, but tears blurred her vision. She held out her hands.

"Here, let me get that off of you." He pulled a knife from his boot and cut the ropes.

She rubbed her chafed wrists and rolled her aching shoulder. Quinn lifted her in his arms, and she looped one arm around his broad shoulders.

"You scared me half to death—once I got over being angry with you."

Sarah blinked. "Why were you angry?"

He pursed his lips. "Because you never told me about your uncle."

"Oh. I tried to, but you didn't seem to believe my story about how I ended up in jail. I was afraid you wouldn't believe the gold tale either."

Quinn looked up for a moment then back at her. His face was inches from hers. "I'm sorry, Sarah."

She brushed her hand along his jaw, feeling the stubble of his day-old beard. He closed his eyes as she fiddled with his hair that ran along his collar.

"Sarah," he ground out the words on a growl. "You sure know how to drive a man crazy."

His eyes opened, and a fire blazed in them that took her breath away. He cupped the back of her head and brought her mouth to his. His kiss was one of promise and it left her breathless. His mouth roamed over her cheeks and eyes, then returned to claim her mouth again.

Too soon, he pulled away, his breathing ragged. "When we get back home, we're going to have a talk about this marriage in name only stuff."

Sarah smiled and stroked his bristly jaw. "It was your idea."

"I know. I can be an idiot at times."

Sarah placed a finger on his warm lips. "Never say that. You're my hero. You've rescued me twice, and I'd love nothing more than to be your wife in every way."

His lips found hers again, and he let her know that he felt the same way.

epilogue

"I cannot believe you two met in jail." Anna clapped her hands and grinned at her husband. "Can you imagine that, Brett?"

Anna's handsome husband shook his head. "Female jail-birds must run in the family."

His wife smacked him on the arm as the other adults in the parlor laughed. "I was only in jail because of you."

"That was the only way to keep you still." Brett's eyes twinkled, and he picked up his coffee cup, dodging his wife's playful smack again.

Sarah liked Quinn's sister and brother-in-law the moment she met them, and Anna pulled her into a hug, saying she was so happy to have another sister. Sarah sat on the sofa beside her husband, her hand in his. She was still uncomfortable with showing affection when others were around, but she was learning to accept it.

Martha yawned and stretched her arms out in front of her. "Tomorrow's a big day. We should all go to bed soon."

Brett stood from the side chair he'd been sitting in and crossed the three feet to his wife in one long step. He held out his hand, and she allowed him to assist her up, her eyes twinkling. Sarah knew just how she felt. Now that she was completely in love with Quinn, it was hard not to smile at him all the time.

Anna wrapped her arm around her husband. "Before we go to bed, there's something we'd like to tell you." She glanced up at Brett and he nodded, a proud smile on his face. "We're going to have a baby."

Martha squealed so loud that Sarah jumped. She hoped the children didn't awaken, because they'd been so excited about Sarah and Quinn's second wedding—a real wedding—that they could hardly go to sleep. Both children knew the significance, and that it meant they would never have to leave the Rocking M.

Quinn dropped Sarah's hand and jumped to his feet. He wrapped Martha and his sister both in a big hug and shook his brother-in-law's hand. "Congratulations! Do you think you might have twins?"

Anna patted her stomach. "Could be. It's early yet, and I'm already starting to show, not that you can tell with all these petticoats I'm wearing."

Sarah's cheeks warmed at Anna's casual reference to her body in mixed company. How long would it be before she and Quinn could make a similar announcement? Ever since her uncle and his gang had been captured last week, Quinn had slept in the bunkhouse. He wanted a new wedding and a fresh start for them—the same thing that Sarah had hoped for, and tomorrow was that day. She quivered at the thought of being Quinn's wife in all ways, couldn't wait to show him how much she loved him.

Anna yawned. "Grandma's right, this baby needs its rest." She turned to Sarah. "Welcome to the family, again. I'm looking forward to getting to know the woman who managed to lasso my big brother."

Brett wrapped his arm around his wife and guided her out of the room.

Martha gave Sarah a hug. "See you two in the morning, though I doubt I'll sleep a wink. You'll make such a lovely bride, dear. And I'm so happy that you and this hooligan grandson of mine are taking your vows again now that you've fallen in love." She squeezed Quinn's hand and pulled him down so she could kiss his cheek. "Good night, you two.

Don't stay up too late."

As soon as she disappeared down the hallway, Quinn pulled Sarah into his arms. His kiss was warm and almost desperate. All too soon, he pulled away. "Do you have any idea how much I love you, Mrs. McFarland?"

Sarah couldn't help smiling and patted his chest. "If it's anything like what I feel for you, then I do."

Quinn heaved a satisfied sigh. "Do you feel like taking a quick trip out to the barn?"

Sarah lifted one brow. "What's in the barn that can't wait until tomorrow?"

Her husband's dark eyes danced with mischievousness. "Come with me, and you'll see."

She nodded, and they walked hand-in-hand out the door. A thousand stars shone bright against the inky sky like tiny lights, but even they dimmed in comparison to the light warming her chest. How was it possible to be so happy? *Thank You, heavenly Father, for making this possible. For sticking me in jail so Quinn could rescue me. And thank You for my husband and his family.*

The barn door creaked open, and Quinn dropped her hand to light the lantern. Sleepy horses ignored them as they walked down the dirt aisle. Quinn stopped at the last stall, and a familiar gray head peered over the gate. Sarah caught her breath and looked up at her husband. His wide grin made him even more handsome, and he shrugged.

"Mary Severson is doing much better, but she doesn't want to ride anymore and has decided to stick to a buggy. Her father decided to sell her horse so it wouldn't be a reminder of the day she got shot." Quinn shuffled his feet and stared at the ground, then peeked at her as if embarrassed. "I just thought that since this horse brought you to Medora—to me—that you might like to have her for a wedding present."

Sarah gasped and threw her arms around his waist. "Oh,

yes, I love the mare. Thank you so much." He pulled her tight against him and kissed the top of her head. After a moment she pulled away. "But I didn't get you a wedding present."

Quinn's smiled turned roguish. "You can give me my present tomorrow night."

Sarah's eyes widened and a warmth rushed to her cheeks. "Thank you for the horse. She's a perfect gift."

He leaned down and kissed her again. Sarah knew she'd found her home. It wasn't a farmhouse or a cabin, but a place next to her husband. Next to Quinn. Wherever he was, that was home.

❧

The sun shone brightly through the stained glass windows of the little church, painting everything it touched in a rainbow of color. A small group of ranch hands, townsfolk, and family had gathered to see Sarah and Quinn married—again.

She peered over her shoulder, and Quinn's sister waved at her. She was so glad that Anna and Brett had been able to attend the wedding. A telegram arrived from Adam and Mariah, sending their regrets from California, best wishes, and the promise to spend the winter at the Rocking M.

Even Sheriff Jones had given them a surprise wedding gift in the form of an official pardon. The gang that had robbed the Medora bank had been captured in Wyoming when they tried to rob a train filled with soldiers. One man had confessed to the Medora robbery and several others in exchange for a lighter sentence. At least Quinn could marry her knowing she was completely innocent of the crimes she'd once been accused of.

Sarah held a small bouquet of flowers tied with long ribbons that draped over the same Bible that Quinn's mother had used when she was married. It would always be special to her. She peeked at her husband and warm tumbleweeds swirled inside her, making her arms and legs go weak. She clung to his arm as he promised to love, cherish, and honor her—"till death do us part."

Beth giggled and squirmed on Sarah's left, looking pretty in her new dress and shoes. Ryan stood next to Quinn, dressed reluctantly in new trousers and shirt. Sarah's only regret was that her parents weren't there—that her father never got to walk her down the aisle. And that her wayward uncle would probably spend the rest of his life in prison.

"Sarah Jane Oakley, do you take this man to be your lawfully wedded husband?"

She grinned up at Quinn. "Oh, yes, I sure do."

His eyes twinkled with delight, and a soft smile danced on his lips. He squeezed her hand tight, so different than the last time they were married.

The plump minister grinned. "By the powers vested in me by God and the state of North Dakota, I now pronounce you man and wife."

Quinn's grin lit up his whole face. "I intend to kiss you this time—to make up for last time." He bent toward her, without waiting on the minister to say the words.

He thoroughly kissed her until the minister coughed.

"Yuck," Ryan called out.

Quinn grinned against her lips. "Is that good enough, wife?"

Sarah shook her head. "It will do for now, but I think you can do better. I know you can."

His eyes twinkled and he nodded.

"Let me present to you Mr. and Mrs. Quinton James McFarland."

The ranch hands whooped and tossed their hats in the air. Grandma fanned herself and reached out for Anna's hand. The small crowd of townsfolk clapped and cheered.

Sarah walked down the short aisle on her husband's arm. He was more than she could ever have hoped for. Quinn hadn't been looking for a wife, and she hadn't wanted a husband, but God had other ideas. He'd given her a man to love and had provided a wonderful home for her family. She looked at the image of Jesus in the colorful window on the side of the church. *Thank You, Lord, for Your bountiful blessings!*

A Letter To Our Readers

Dear Reader:

In order that we might better contribute to your reading enjoyment, we would appreciate your taking a few minutes to respond to the following questions. We welcome your comments and read each form and letter we receive. When completed, please return to the following:

Fiction Editor
Heartsong Presents
PO Box 719
Uhrichsville, Ohio 44683

1. Did you enjoy reading *Straight for the Heart* by Vickie McDonough?
   ☐ Very much! I would like to see more books by this author!
   ☐ Moderately. I would have enjoyed it more if

   _____

   _____

   _____

2. Are you a member of **Heartsong Presents**? ☐ Yes ☐ No
   If no, where did you purchase this book? _____

   _____

3. How would you rate, on a scale from 1 (poor) to 5 (superior), the cover design? _____

4. On a scale from 1 (poor) to 10 (superior), please rate the following elements.

   ____ Heroine   ____ Plot
   ____ Hero   ____ Inspirational theme
   ____ Setting   ____ Secondary characters

5. These characters were special because? _____

_____

_____

6. How has this book inspired your life? _____

_____

_____

7. What settings would you like to see covered in future
   Heartsong Presents books? _____

_____

_____

8. What are some inspirational themes you would like to see
   treated in future books? _____

_____

_____

9. Would you be interested in reading other **Heartsong
   Presents** titles? ❏ Yes   ❏ No

10. Please check your age range:
    ❏ Under 18   ❏ 18-24
    ❏ 25-34   ❏ 35-45
    ❏ 46-55   ❏ Over 55

Name _____

Occupation _____

Address _____

City, State, Zip _____

Beloved Counterfeit

*Y*ou'll be swept away by this enticing story of a reformed sinner, a widowed preacher, and a lecherous pirate.

Historical, paperback, 320 pages, 5³⁄₁₆" x 8"

_____

Presents

Great Inspirational Romance at a Great Price!

Heartsong Presents books are inspirational romances in contemporary and historical settings, designed to give you an enjoyable, spirit-lifting reading experience. You can choose wonderfully written titles from some of today's best authors like Wanda E. Brunstetter, Mary Conneuly, Susan Page Davis, Cathy Marie Hake, Joyce Livingston, and many others.

When ordering quantities less than twelve, above titles are $2.97 each.
Not all titles may be available at time of order.